P9-DNL-370

Marion County Public Library
321 Monroe Street
Fairmont, WV 26554

From the Pages of
The Waste Land and Other Poems

Let us go then, you and I,
When the evening is spread out against the sky
Like a patient etherised upon a table;
Let us go, through certain half-deserted streets,
The muttering retreats
Of restless nights in one-night cheap hotels
And sawdust restaurants with oyster-shells:
Streets that follow like a tedious argument
Of insidious intent
To lead you to an overwhelming question . . .
Oh, do not ask, 'What is it?'
Let us go and make our visit.

> (from 'The Love Song of J. Alfred Prufrock,' page 9)

And I must borrow every changing shape
To find expression . . . dance, dance
Like a dancing bear,
Cry like a parrot, chatter like an ape.
Let us take the air, in a tobacco trance—

> (from 'Portrait of a Lady,' page 17)

The woman keeps the kitchen, makes tea,
Sneezes at evening, poking the peevish gutter.
            I an old man,
A dull head among windy spaces.

> (from 'Gerontion,' page 37)

April is the cruellest month, breeding
Lilacs out of the dead land, mixing
Memory and desire, stirring

JUN   2007

321 MONROE STREET
FAIRMONT, WV 26554

Dull roots with spring rain.
Winter kept us warm, covering
Earth in forgetful snow, feeding
A little life with dried tubers.

(from 'The Waste Land,' page 65)

Here is no water but only rock
Rock and no water and the sandy road
The road winding above among the mountains
Which are mountains of rock without water
If there were water we should stop and drink
Amongst the rock one cannot stop or think
Sweat is dry and feet are in the sand
If there were only water amongst the rock
Dead mountain mouth of carious teeth that cannot spit
Here one can neither stand nor lie nor sit
There is not even silence in the mountains
But dry sterile thunder without rain
There is not even solitude in the mountains
But red sullen faces sneer and snarl
From doors of mudcracked houses.

(from 'The Waste Land,' page 78)

These fragments I have shored against my ruins.

(from 'The Waste Land,' page 81)

THE WASTE LAND
AND OTHER POEMS

T. S. Eliot

With an Introduction and Notes
by Randy Malamud

George Stade
Consulting Editorial Director

BARNES & NOBLE CLASSICS
NEW YORK

𝓑

BARNES & NOBLE CLASSICS

NEW YORK

Published by Barnes & Noble Books
122 Fifth Avenue
New York, NY 10011

www.barnesandnoble.com/classics

Prufrock and Other Observations was first published in 1917, *Poems 1920*
in 1919, and *The Waste Land* in 1922.

Published in 2005 by Barnes & Noble Classics with new Introduction,
Notes, Biography, Chronology, Inspired By, Comments & Questions,
and For Further Reading.

Introduction, Notes, and For Further Reading
Copyright © 2005 by Randy Malamud.

Note on T. S. Eliot, The World of T. S. Eliot and His Poetry,
Inspired by T. S. Eliot and *The Waste Land*, and Comments & Questions
Copyright © 2004 by Barnes & Noble, Inc.

All rights reserved. No part of this publication may be reproduced or
transmitted in any form or by any means, electronic or mechanical,
including photocopy, recording, or any information storage and
retrieval system, without the prior written permission of the publisher.

Barnes & Noble Classics and the Barnes & Noble Classics colophon
are trademarks of Barnes & Noble, Inc.

The Waste Land and Other Poems
ISBN-13: 978-1-59308-279-6
ISBN-10: 1-59308-279-7
LC Control Number 2004112106

Produced and published in conjunction with:
Fine Creative Media, Inc.
322 Eighth Avenue
New York, NY 10001

Michael J. Fine, President and Publisher

Printed in the United States of America
QM
3 5 7 9 10 8 6 4

b14661998

T. S. Eliot

Poet, critic, playwright, editor, and Nobel laureate, Thomas Stearns Eliot was born on September 26, 1888, to Henry Ware and Charlotte Stearns Eliot. The family shared a double allegiance to Missouri and New England—Eliot's grandfather founded the Unitarian Church of St. Louis; his mother's family were settlers in the first Massachusetts Bay Colony. Young Eliot's temperament tended toward the reserve of his New England heritage, and summers spent on the Massachusetts coast would later inform his poems.

After early private schooling, Eliot followed his brother to Harvard University, where he joined the Signet literary society and studied a remarkable array of subjects. Deeply influenced by the Symbolist movement, he published his first poems in the Harvard *Advocate*. After receiving B.A. and M.A. degrees, Eliot traveled to Paris, studied at the Sorbonne, and frequented the salons of Europe's most influential thinkers and artists. He returned for graduate work to Harvard, where he pursued a doctorate in philosophy with such renowned professors as Bertrand Russell, George Santayana, and William James. After three years of intense study, including courses in Hebrew and Sanskrit, Eliot won a fellowship to Marburg, Germany. World War I cut short his time there, and after a brief tenure at Oxford he was taken under the wing of avant-garde literary figure Ezra Pound.

Beginning with the publication of *Prufrock and Other Observations* in 1917, Eliot's reputation as a major poet grew during the postwar years. But his marriage to the physically and emotionally troubled Vivien Haigh-Wood precipitated a nervous breakdown in 1921. While recuperating in Margate, England, and Lausanne, Switzerland, Eliot composed *The Waste Land* (1922). Ezra Pound was entrusted with editing the unwieldy manuscript, and his decisive, even radical changes did much to hone the work. When it was published by *The Dial* in 1922, the modernist masterpiece changed the way poetry was both read and composed.

Eliot juggled his writing with work at Lloyds Bank and editorial positions at *The Egoist* and *The Criterion*, and later at the publishing house Faber and Faber. In 1927 he became a British citizen and joined the Anglican Church. After he separated from Vivien in 1932, he produced a tremendous amount of work: creative writing, literary criticism, and a series of university lectures.

Eliot's many essays on culture, language, and literature greatly influenced twentieth-century criticism. In 'Hamlet and His Problems' (1919) he introduced the notion of the 'objective correlative'—an objective fact or circumstance that correlates with an inner feeling—as part of his argument for precision of language. In 'The Metaphysical Poets' (1921) he defined 'dissociation of sensibility' as a break between feeling and thought that had occurred as English poetry was written in the eighteenth and nineteenth centuries; Eliot advocated the reuniting of emotion and intellect in works of literature.

Eliot was also a playwright; among his major dramatic works are *Murder in the Cathedral, The Family Reunion, The Cocktail Party*, and *The Elder Statesman*.

Shortly after the publication of his second masterpiece, *Four Quartets* (1943), Eliot received the Nobel Prize in Literature, as well as countless awards and honorary doctorates. *Four Quartets* was the last of Eliot's major poetry, but he remained occupied with writing for the rest of his life. He published more than 600 works in the course of his career, and worked at Faber and Faber until his death. Personal happiness finally came with his marriage to Valerie Fletcher in 1957. T. S. Eliot died in London in 1965 and was buried in East Coker, with the epitaph, 'In my beginning is my end. In my end is my beginning,' taken from *Four Quartets*.

Contents

The World of T. S. Eliot
and His Poetry

1888 Thomas Stearns Eliot is born on September 26, in St. Louis, Missouri, to Henry Ware and Charlotte Stearns Eliot. The youngest of seven children, Eliot is brought up in a prosperous household. His grandfather, William Greenleaf Eliot, had attended Harvard Divinity School before heading west to found the first Unitarian church in St. Louis.

1889– Thomas is educated at Smith Academy in St. Louis. The
1904 family spends summers in Gloucester, Massachusetts, where the young boy learns to sail and fish; these summers instill in him a love of the sea and a New England sensibility. William James's *The Principles of Psychology* (1890), Oscar Wilde's *The Picture of Dorian Gray* (1890), Sigmund Freud's *The Interpretation of Dreams* (1900), and Henry James's *The Golden Bowl* (1904) are published. Queen Victoria dies (1901).

1905 Eliot attends Milton Academy near Boston for one year.

1906– He joins his older brother, Henry, at Harvard (1906). While
1910 an undergraduate, Eliot studies with Irving Babbitt and George Santayana; his academic interests are wide-ranging and diverse. The Symbolist movement deeply influences the young writer. He contributes poems to the Harvard literary magazine, *The Advocate*, and joins the Signet literary society. While playing the part of Mr. Woodhouse in a production of *Emma*, he begins a romantic relationship with Emily Hale. He earns both B.A. (1909) and M.A. (1910) degrees. E. M. Forster's *Howards End* is published (1910).

1910– Eliot attends the Sorbonne in Paris. There he meets a variety
1911 of French artists and intellectuals, and develops a close friendship with Jean Verdenal, to whom he will dedicate *Prufrock and Other Observations*. Eliot writes several enduring

poems during this year spent abroad, including 'Prufrock,' 'La Figlia che Piange,' 'Preludes,' 'Portrait of a Lady,' and 'Rhapsody on a Windy Night.'

1911– Eliot pursues a Ph.D. in philosophy at Harvard. His professors,
1914   including Bertrand Russell, George Santayana, and William James, are some of the most distinguished philosophers of the twentieth century. Bertrand Russell's *The Problems of Philosophy* (1912) is published.

1914   While Eliot is studying in Germany, World War I begins. He takes up residence at Merton College, Oxford University, but his plans to pursue a Ph.D. are cut short by the war. In London a friend shows Eliot's poetry to Ezra Pound, and their legendary collaboration begins. James Joyce's *Dubliners* is published. Eliot will later edit Joyce's *Ulysses* for serial publication.

1915– 'Prufrock' is published in *Poetry* and *Blast* magazines. An
1916   Oxford friend introduces Eliot to Vivien Haigh-Wood. Eliot's family is concerned because of Vivien's history of instability. Struggling to make a living, Eliot teaches school, writes reviews, and does editing for various publications. Although he and Vivien will not travel to the United States because of the war, he finishes and submits his doctoral dissertation, 'Experience and the Objects of Knowledge in the Philosophy of F. H. Bradley.' Ezra Pound's *Cathay* (1915) is published. In 1916 Joyce's *A Portrait of the Artist as a Young Man* and C. G. Jung's *Psychology of the Unconscious* are published.

1917   Eliot's knowledge of languages secures him a post with Lloyds Bank. *Prufrock and Other Observations* is published by *The Egoist*. Eliot begins editing for the journal and associating with the Bloomsbury group and other philosophers and writers.

1919   'Tradition and the Individual Talent' (1919) appears in *The Egoist*.

1920   *Poems 1920* and a book of criticism, *The Sacred Wood*, are published. Increasing tensions with his mentally ill wife cause Eliot tremendous stress. Katherine Mansfield's *Bliss*, Edith Wharton's *The Age of Innocence*, and D. H. Lawrence's *Women in Love* are published.

1921   Eliot suffers a mental breakdown. To recuperate, he travels to Margate and then to a sanitarium in Lausanne, Switzerland. The rest proves restorative and fruitful: Eliot writes his groundbreaking *The Waste Land* while abroad. Ezra Pound, whose *Poems, 1918–1921* is published this year, brilliantly edits *The Waste Land* when Eliot travels through Paris.

1922   Eliot receives a literary award from *The Dial*, the journal that publishes *The Waste Land* later this year. Eliot founds the journal *The Criterion*, which he will edit until 1939. James Joyce's *Ulysses* is published.

1923   W. B. Yeats receives the Nobel Prize for Literature.

1924   Thomas Mann's *The Magic Mountain* is published.

1925   *Poems, 1909–1925*, which includes 'The Hollow Men,' is published. Eliot becomes an editor for the publishing house Faber and Gwyer (later Faber and Faber). F. Scott Fitzgerald's *The Great Gatsby* and the first sections of Ezra Pound's *Cantos* are published.

1926   Eliot gives the Clark Lectures at Cambridge University.

1927   He becomes a British citizen and joins the Anglican Church. Virginia Woolf's *To the Lighthouse* and Bertrand Russell's *Why I Am Not a Christian* are published.

1928   *For Lancelot Andrewes* is published. Evelyn Waugh's *Decline and Fall* and Yeats's *The Tower* are published.

1929   *Dante* is published. William Faulkner's *The Sound and the Fury* and Robert Graves's *Goodbye to All That* are published.

1930   *Ash-Wednesday* is published. W. H. Auden's *Poems* is published.

1932–   *Selected Essays, 1917–1932* (1932) is published, as is *Sweeney*
1933   *Agonistes: Fragments of an Aristophanic Melodrama* (1932). After years of anguish and tumult, Eliot separates from Vivien, although he will not divorce her because of his religious beliefs. He delivers the Charles Eliot Norton Lectures at Harvard; they are published as *The Use of Poetry and the Use of Criticism* (1933). Aldous Huxley's *Brave New World* (1932) and Yeats's *Collected Poems* are published (1933).

1934   *After Strange Gods*, the collection of lectures Eliot delivered in 1933 at the University of Virginia, is published, as is *Elizabethan Essays*. The church pageant *The Rock* is performed and published. Eliot reestablishes contact with his college love, Emily Hale. Ezra Pound's *ABC of Reading* is published.

1935   *Murder in the Cathedral* is performed and published.

1936   *Collected Poems, 1909–1935*, including 'Burnt Norton,' is published.

1937   Wallace Stevens's *The Man with the Blue Guitar* is published.

1938   Vivien is committed to the mental hospital Northumberland House.

1939   With war impending, Eliot ceases publication of *The Criterion*. *The Family Reunion* is performed and published, as are *The Idea of a Christian Society* and *Old Possum's Book of Practical Cats*. James Joyce's *Finnegans Wake* is published. World War II begins.

1940   *East Coker* is published; the poem's title is the name of the village in Somerset, England, from which Eliot's ancestors had emigrated to America in the 1600s.

1941   *The Dry Salvages* is published.

1942   *Little Gidding* is published.

1943   *Four Quartets*—an edition in one volume of 'Burnt Norton,' 'East Coker,' 'The Dry Salvages,' and 'Little Gidding'—is published.

1945   George Orwell's *Animal Farm* and Bertrand Russell's *A History of Western Philosophy* are published.

1947   Vivien Eliot dies.

1948   Eliot receives the Nobel Prize for Literature. *Notes Towards the Definition of Culture* is published.

1949   *The Cocktail Party* is performed. Arthur Miller's *Death of a Salesman* receives the Pulitzer Prize.

1950   *Poems Written in Early Youth* and *The Cocktail Party* are published.

1951   *Poetry and Drama* is published.

1952   Samuel Beckett's *En attendant Godot* (*Waiting for Godot*) is published.

1953–   *The Confidential Clerk* is performed and then published.
1954

1957 Eliot marries Valerie Fletcher. *On Poetry and Poets* is published.

1958– *The Elder Statesman* is performed and then published.
1959

1963 *Collected Poems, 1909–1962* is published.

1965 Thomas Stearns Eliot dies in London on January 4. His ashes are taken to East Coker. In accordance with his wishes, his epitaph includes lines from *Four Quartets*: 'In my beginning is my end. In my end is my beginning.'

Introduction

We present in this volume T. S. Eliot's first three published poetic volumes: two slight and rather odd collections of a dozen poems each, and then (in Ezra Pound's words) 'the longest poem in the English langwidge,' *The Waste Land*. The poems here were conceived and begun in 1910, and published in 1917, 1919–1920, and 1922. In the wake of these publications, Eliot became a profoundly important voice in modern literary and cultural affairs, a position he would sustain over the next half century.

Eliot was, technically, an American. Born in St. Louis in 1888, he escaped the Midwest for the East Coast when he matriculated to Harvard University in 1906. Thinking that perhaps Cambridge, Massachusetts, could satisfy his intellectual and cultural appetites, he stayed there to complete his B.A. in 1909 and M.A. in 1910; he embarked upon (and essentially completed) his doctoral work in philosophy, but by the time he was deep into his graduate training, he became convinced that even the esoteric Harvard atmosphere was insufficient for his needs, and he abandoned America for Europe. He went to Oxford in 1914, and ended up settling in England for the rest of his life.

Eliot cemented his English connection by marrying, precipitously, an English woman, Vivien Haigh-Wood. This alliance proved unsuccessful in every way. The misogynistic strains of 'The Love Song of J. Alfred Prufrock,' 'Rhapsody on a Windy Night,' 'Hysteria,' 'Sweeney Erect,' and 'Lune de Miel'—poems that become profoundly troubled when women or even the thoughts of women are proximate—probably illuminate Eliot's difficulties in his marital relationship. But Eliot displaced the unhappiness of his private life with the increasing success of his public career. He rose through the ranks of the preeminent London publishing firm Faber & Faber, where he grew into the figure that he had always longed to be: an influential English poet and critic. Recordings of his poetry readings reveal a studied, careful, august, and slightly doleful English accent that he acquired as the *pièce de resistance* in his transformation from a midwestern American to a cosmopolitan European.

It is tempting to read Eliot's first three collections in the Hegelian mode of thesis, antithesis, and synthesis. *Prufrock and Other Observations* (1917), the first term in this formulation, represents a series of (as the title promises) 'observations'—detached, cynical, and weary (this from a man in his twenties!). Eliot offers a variety of scenes and tableaux—the genteel drawing rooms of 'Portrait of a Lady' and 'Aunt Helen,' the tawdry streetscapes of 'Rhapsody on a Windy Night,' 'Preludes,' and 'Morning at the Window'—in which not much happens, prompting the poetic 'hero' to ratiocinate and intellectualize . . . and again, in this process, not much happens.

The upshot of the speaker's careful observation and deliberation is always anti-climactic, unsatisfying. At the end of a potentially illuminating meeting with Mr. Apollinax in the poem of that title, the speaker clutches desperately and pathetically to discover some meaningful token of the encounter but finally, appraising the milieu that he had hoped would be so rarefied, can say only, absurdly, 'I remember a slice of lemon, and a bitten macaroon.' In all these poems, if there is any conscious insight or action that results from the observations recounted, it is negative and passive: disappointment, deflation, repression, flight.

The poetic narratives, such as they are, are quietly understated and bleakly banal. It is as if the reader is seeing the poem's action from a distance, perhaps because the poet cannot bear to approach the scene any more closely. Prufrock worries: What if a potential friend, 'settling a pillow by her head, / Should say: "That is not what I meant at all. / That is not it, at all." ' Anticipating possible failure, the speaker foregoes any attempt at communion, and the poem ends with self-protective solitude: 'I shall wear white flannel trousers, and walk upon the beach.'

A recent edition of Eliot's notebooks from 1909 to 1917, *Inventions of the March Hare* (edited by Christopher Ricks), generates many fascinating insights into the composition of the early poems. The notebooks illustrate how long Eliot spent carefully working and nurturing the relatively few poems he actually published, and demonstrate the difference between the published work and a considerable number of other attempts, most of which one would classify as juvenilia, that he did not publish.

The notebooks reinforce how carefully Eliot modulated the diction and tenor of this poetry. We see, for example, in a passage from the fourth stanza of 'Rhapsody on a Windy Night,' in which a street-lamp surrealistically speaks of 'the cat which flattens itself in the gutter, / Slips out its tongue / And devours a morsel of rancid butter,' that the word 'rancid' was a late addition. We may surmise that that word carries an especially potent resonance: that it was (as Flaubert would say) *le mot juste*, carrying the connotation that, Eliot judged as he perfected the poem, emphatically conveyed the atmosphere of this scene. In the next stanza, it is a deletion that shows how Eliot conveys the mood: The line that reads 'A washed-out smallpox cracks her face' began, in draft, as 'the hideous scars of a washed-out pox': But Eliot must have decided that it was too heavy-handed and obvious; the more suggestive and understated description is more powerful. The whole milieu is, of course, hideous, but it is more effective if readers infer that instead of the poet explaining it.

The most interesting textual revelation in these notebooks concerns a long section (thirty-nine lines) that originally had been part of 'The Love Song of J. Alfred Prufrock' but was finally suppressed. Eliot called this section 'Prufrock's Pervigilium' (a pervigilium is an all-night vigil), and it describes an experience strikingly more feverish and nervous than the rest of the poem and close in tenor to the spirit of 'Rhapsody on a Windy Night.' Of course, the fact that this section does not appear in the final draft of 'Prufrock' means that it is not, precisely, part of the poem's ambience, but nevertheless it colors our understanding of the character. The fact that such writhing, nauseous madness (as Eliot describes it) pervades the pervigilium that Prufrock might have kept helps readers to appreciate the sublimated tensions in the poem that may otherwise seem unexpected, or exaggerated, or perverse. The dark energies of the 'Pervigilium' suggest how terrifying the world of this quiet, mannerly character might have become.

As antithesis to *Prufrock and Other Observations*, we have *Poems 1920*: highly wrought (overworked and nearly impenetrable, one

might reasonably conclude) and densely allusive. The voice is in-
tellectually haughty, which seems to be another mode of achieving
the distanced isolation that pervaded *Prufrock*. The poems are
wrenched with unstable combinations of classicism and fetid con-
temporary Hobbesian turmoil. What had been a minor strain in
Eliot's first collection—the interiorized angst of 'Hysteria,' the tensely
uncomfortable atmosphere of 'Mr. Apollinax'—blossoms into a full-
blown neurosis in the second. If the poems in *Prufrock* were almost
too simple, those in Eliot's 1920 collection were far too difficult—
and both the simplicity and the difficulty suggest a strategy of eva-
siveness that Eliot employs to avoid what he will finally achieve in
The Waste Land: a direct, honest, realistic appraisal of the condi-
tion of the world around him.

Poems 1920 (published in a nearly identical edition in 1919 as
Poems, and also published under a different title, *Ara Vos Prec*, in
1920) has an offhand but insistent anti-Semitic taint, as Anthony
Julius has convincingly expounded: from the squatting Jew in 'Geron-
tion' to the saggy Chicago Semite in 'Burbank with a Baedeker: Blei-
stein with a Cigar,' from the stereotypically fiduciary Sir Alfred
Mond in 'A Cooking Egg' to the stereotypically voracious and
whorish Rachel *née* Rabinovitch in 'Sweeney Among the Nightin-
gales.' The slurs that resonate in these poems testify to Eliot's in-
creasing disturbance, and probably, as in most cases of prejudice, a
desire to blame 'the other' as a scapegoat for the cultural decadence
and failure of the mainstream, empowered society. The poems here
are philosophical, in a perverse, anti-rational way—exactly what
one might expect from someone who had embraced but then aban-
doned the discipline of philosophy. Eliot's eclectic (and sometimes
disorienting) influences in this collection include Lewis Carroll,
Henry Adams, John Ruskin, French Symbolists, and Jacobean
dramatists, among many others.

Three of the poems feature a character named Sweeney. Eliot
once described him 'as a man who in younger days was perhaps a
pugilist, mildly successful; who then grew older and retired to keep
a pub.' He is meant to evoke, obviously, an Irishman (with all the
class and nationalist prejudices one might expect from an elitist
English perspective) who is coarse and boorish but also, dis-
turbingly, casts a powerful presence: He is a loose cannon, sexually

potent and physically aggressive. He stumbles into Eliot's tableaux and causes a rude disturbance: The quatrain poems attempt to regroup themselves, to adapt to his existence, which they do with a strained, excessive, tenuous classicist intellectualism that sets off Sweeney's character all the more sharply. Sweeney embodies Eliot's obsession, in his 1920 poems, with a visceral figure who is starkly opposed to the demure, repressed, polite (if artificial) society figures that populate *Prufrock*.

In *Prufrock*, the general milieu of the poems was a detailed, specific, urban streetscape: one that seemed typical of London, though actually many of the poems owe more to Eliot's youthful meandering among the byways of Cambridge, Massachusetts. In *Poems 1920*, the atmosphere is more broadly European: There is a wider and richer (but also, certainly, an ironized and perverted) sense of the entire continent, from Brussels to Limoges, from London and Paris to Ravenna, Padua, Milan, and Venice. (In *The Waste Land*, the topography will synthesize these two extremes: The poem traverses both the localized London streets and the more panoramic spectacle of Europe.) Indeed, four of the poems are in French. Editions published during Eliot's lifetime did not include translations accompanying these poems; presumably, he wanted them to remain elusive to a monoglot audience, and if one wanted to read poems in French, then one must simply learn French. Perhaps Eliot wanted to celebrate a sense of cosmopolitan culture by including several works in another language; he was probably also showing off his cultural breadth. Finally, as Samuel Beckett (an Irishman who wrote many of his works in French) discovered, a writer may accomplish certain effects by working in a language that is not his primary tongue: a studied sense of detachment or alienation, perhaps. Disregarding Eliot's resistance to making his French verse accessible to a larger reading audience, the present edition includes English renditions of these poems.

If we regard Eliot's first two collections as thesis/antithesis, then the synthesis was accompanied by (and probably in many ways facilitated by) a personal breakdown in 1921. *The Waste Land* is a record of the poet's collapse, as well as the sign of his recovery. As he traveled back from Switzerland, where he had undergone treatment, to resume his life in England, Eliot left a draft of the poem in Paris for Ezra Pound to edit. The poem records a nervous breakdown, but more importantly it recounts how the poet imposes a sense of order, coherence, and direction on the cacophonous chaos of the breakdown.

Explicitly, the breakdown in *The Waste Land* is meant to be the breakdown of Europe, but increasingly critics have come to realize that it is also the very personal account of Eliot's own psychological distress. In part III, for example, he writes, ' "On Margate Sands. / I can connect / Nothing with nothing." ' The beach at Margate was where Eliot had vacationed, following a friend's advice, in an attempt to avert his breakdown; but the holiday did not ameliorate his situation and prompted him to seek the therapeutic assistance of a Lausanne psychologist, Dr. Henri Vittoz. And when the voice of the poem states (in an unusual first-person address) in line 182, 'By the waters of Leman I sat down and wept . . .' Eliot is describing the simple, powerful nadir of his breakdown: Leman is the old name for Lake Geneva, which Lausanne overlooks. Although Eliot always resisted autobiographical readings of art, the poem inescapably invites such readings. In the closing lines, when Eliot writes 'These fragments I have shored against my ruins,' it seems impossible not to read that as a description of how Eliot's embrace and desperate association of the shards that comprise the poem have helped to stave off his psychological 'ruins.' The act of assembling these pieces of the European cultural tradition served as a bulwark against the intellectual collapse—in both his public and private worlds— that seemed so imminent.

On the national level, the breakdown Eliot envisioned was a consequence of the state of Europe during and after the Great War. More personally, the poem can be read as an account from the trenches of a poet who, though he didn't actually fight in that war, fought and survived his own metaphorical war. (Critics have speculated that Virginia Woolf's Septimus Smith, the shell-shocked poet manqué in *Mrs. Dalloway*, was at least loosely inspired by her erstwhile friend Tom.)

The Waste Land achieves a synthesis between the free-floating observations of *Prufrock* and the anguished, surreal pretensions of *Poems 1920*. The philosophical/intellectual praxis of Eliot's modern epic is less gratuitous, and more pragmatic, than what he pro-pounded in his previous collection — still difficult and harsh, cer-tainly, but in a way that lent itself (at least for Eliot's initiates, his devotees) to solving, working through. If *Poems 1920* was (and was meant to be) off-putting, *The Waste Land* was somehow, despite itself, addictively compelling. The themes, the tropes, the images, the aesthetic that Eliot created in that poem are still going strong, inescapably etched into our cultural consciousness nearly a cen-tury later. (For example, it is virtually impossible to read any newspaper in any April without a headline recalling that it is 'the cruelest month.') Eliot postulated that the modern landscape looked harsh, hostile, crazy, fragmented, with the monuments of the past tormenting us amid our present unworthiness and inade-quacy, and apparently he was right.

A first-time reader confronted with *The Waste Land* must deter-mine, at the outset, how to read the poem: how to assimilate it and make sense of it. It is, of course, 'modern,' so one approaches it with the same understanding of modern aesthetics that one brings to Pi-casso's cubism, or Stravinsky's symphonies, or Diaghilev's dance. One allows that the apparent chaos of the work, the difficulty, the excess, is in some way mimetic of the dazzling and sometimes in-coherent world outside; and also that things will not be presented in a neat, clear narrative structure, because anything too conven-tional or too easily accessible would be consequently trite — one must work hard to glean important insights from the modern zeit-geist. Modernists believed that the more complex a text is, the more likely it is to do justice to the complexity of the world outside, a world that in the space of one generation is awakening to cinema, telephones, automobiles, airplanes, world war, and so forth.

The poem suggests many schemes or models — probably far too many — that offer aids to comprehension. Some of these come from Eliot's own critical apparatus: The notes at the end of the poem, for example, promise insights. The endnotes were not included with the first two periodical publications of the poem — in *The Criterion* (London) in October 1922 and in *The Dial* (New York) the next month; they appeared only with the first book edition. Eliot once said that the publishers of this edition 'wanted a larger volume and the notes were the only available matter,' and in a 1957 lecture he referred to them as a 'remarkable exposition of bogus scholarship.' In fact, the notes vary greatly in relevance and usefulness.

The notes to lines 218 and 412 seem to be tremendously important keys to the poem, in terms of explaining how readers may resolve the confusing medley of perspectives and consciousness (Tiresias is 'the most important personage in the poem, uniting all the rest,' Eliot writes in his note to line 218, and his comment at line 412 gives a brief but incisive explanation of how Bradleyan philosophy—the subject of his dissertation—informs the sensory experience of the poem). The references to various sources show how intertextually Eliot composed, and how he wants us to read; several notes reference other passages in the poem, giving a sense of its internal connections and letting readers know that it is important to make these kind of associations—to remember what has gone on before, and how we might organize and categorize the array of images and themes that the poem presents.

On the other hand, some of the notes seem pointless, such as the one at line 46 that begins 'I am not familiar with the exact constitution of the Tarot pack of cards . . .'; and some are unexpectedly personal: The note to line 68 coyly reads, 'A phenomenon which I have often noticed' (providing, at least in a small way, another piece of evidence for reading the poem as an autobiographical account). Certainly the references to Jessie Weston and Sir James Frazer at the top of the endnotes are informative: They have spurred numerous critical commentaries about how the poem may be read as a kind of quest, along the lines of Weston's study of the Grail legend, or as an anthropological account of independent but congruent myths, as Frazer described in his masterwork *The Golden Bough*.

At one point in my career, I actually read the poem while stopping to consult every reference that Eliot cites. I cannot say that this exercise necessarily helped me understand the poem better, but I did spend a great deal of time pursuing an eclectic and useful course of reading as prescribed by Professor Eliot, and perhaps this was precisely the point: to make sure that readers experienced a large dose of other works in the more conventional literary canon, by Ovid and Baudelaire and Goldsmith and Verlaine, to mitigate the experience of reading just *The Waste Land*, just this modernist spasm. I think Eliot intended that people not read the poem in isolation, because it makes sense only to the extent that we appreciate it as being in dialogue with the vast tradition that preceded it. Eliot makes this point in one of his best-known essays, 'Tradition and the Individual Talent' (see 'For Further Reading'), where he writes, 'No poet, no artist of any art, has his complete meaning alone. His significance, his appreciation is the appreciation of his relation to the dead poets and artists. You cannot value him alone; you must set him, for contrast and comparison, among the dead.' And he makes the point that not only does the older work inform the new, but also vice versa: 'What happens when a new work of art is created is something that happens simultaneously to all the works of art which preceded it. The existing monuments form an ideal order among themselves, which is modified by the introduction of the new (the really new) work of art among them.'

When one reads *The Waste Land* through the lens of its myriad literary allusions and echoes, Chaucer, Shakespeare, and Dante appear as the most prominent touchstones; the reader is invited to make connections, and to compare Eliot's aesthetic to those of his predecessors. The opening lines invoke, obviously, the beginning of the General Prologue to the *Canterbury Tales*. For Chaucer, in his dazzling sociocultural survey, April and its rains were soothing, nurturing, regenerative. The cycles of nature, of seasons, of social ceremonies, were all fecund with the possibility of generating new narratives. Eliot's ironic reiteration of Chaucer's April suggests an antithetical, cynical outlook on all the cultural observations that were so profusely interesting to the fourteenth-century poet. If Chaucer's work stands as an opening bookend to the literary tradition, Eliot seems to be positioning his own contribution to the tradition as the closing bookend, the poem to end all poems. The pilgrims' fresh, vibrant, profusely detailed personalities that Chaucer paraded in the General Prologue become, in Eliot's hands, more stinted and interiorized; elusive, troubled, and socially dubious.

Chaucer's cast of characters was brimming with stories: performances of self-expression, or anagnorisis, or morality, or cultural criticism. If we regard *The Waste Land* as Eliot's General Prologue, though, it is difficult to imagine what sorts of narratives might ensue from, say, Madame Sosostris or Mr. Eugenides or Mrs. Porter or Marie. For Chaucer, the point of the stories was to pass the time on the long journey to Canterbury: to accompany the spiritual quest and the communal act of devotion it embodied with the more popular, personal, pluralistic strain that the stories would foster. In *The Waste Land*, if it seems that the narratives are pervasively muted ('I could not / Speak, and my eyes failed'; 'Why do you never speak'; 'I made no comment'), perhaps that is meant to suggest that there is no spiritual pilgrimage to be undertaken comparable to Chaucer's (so there's no point offering up any stories to pass the time on the journey that there's no point in taking anyhow), or that if such a quest is conceivable, then the cultural tradition at hand, bankrupt in the wake of early-twentieth-century chaos, has no stories to accompany the quest. (Perhaps not in English, but in another tongue? Perhaps that is why there are so many languages in the poem, and why the culminating mantras appear in Sanskrit rather than in any European tongue.) The cruelty of Eliot's April, as contrasted with the sweetness of Chaucer's, reflects the modernist angst at coming around once again to a season that has traditionally been associated with rebirth and resurrection, but finding the task at present horribly unpromising.

Shakespeare and Dante are also frequently evoked in the poem. Eliot wrote numerous critical essays about both of them, explaining his preference for the clear, devout certainty of Dante's voice over what he saw as Shakespeare's muddled, polymorphous aesthetic. Eliot believed a great poet is an amanuensis of his times, and Dante was fortunate to have lived in an era that Eliot found ideologically and intellectually more coherent than the Elizabethan age. (As for what he thought about his own time: The nervous, schizophrenic entropy of *The Waste Land* demonstrates how disappointed he was with the cultural incoherence of his contemporary society. A culture gets what it deserves.)

In his 1929 essay *Dante*, Eliot wrote, 'Gradually we come to admit that Shakespeare understands a greater extent and variety of human life than Dante; but that Dante understands deeper degrees of degradation and higher degrees of exaltation.' And thus, Eliot concludes, 'Shakespeare gives the greatest *width* of human passion; Dante the greatest altitude and greatest depth.'

Within the schema of *The Waste Land*, this suggests that Dante is the more valuable guide. The *width* of human passion in the poem seems ultimately unsatisfying and ineffective: Of the numerous potential passionate engagements—ranging from Marie and the arch-duke in part I to 'you and I together' walking in part V— few last more than a half-dozen lines. The accumulation of these scenes fails to advance communality or commonweal, suggesting the insubstantiality of a Shakespearean 'width of passion.' The poem's more effective movement, instead, describes a journey from the depths of human passion—wintry hibernation, barren and mechanical lust—to the altitude of the clouds over Himavant, where the voice of the thunder broaches guidance and peace.

The Dante–Shakespeare binary is closely associated with an important thematic opposition in the poem, fire versus water. Passages with Dantean resonances invoke the intensities of the fiery torment of *Inferno*, while the Shakespearean allusions tend to recall water. It might seem that the Shakespearean water would be a desirable antidote to the dryness of the waste land, but in fact such water always proves delusory in its potentially nurturing effect. At the beginning of part II, for example, Eliot invokes Cleopatra's image as the magnificent, seductive queen is seen floating down the Nile— the barge in her queenly procession 'burnt on the water' as Shakespeare put it, provocatively uniting fire and water; but Eliot undercuts this imagery as his modern Cleopatra merely 'glowed on the marble.' Eliot rejects the possibility that fire and water can be so easily reconciled, and he realizes that Cleopatra's ultimate failure was her misperception of the reality of water. Her poor leadership is reflected in Antony's ill-fated decision (compounded by her whimsical and arbitrary nautical strategy) to wage war on the water rather than on land. Shakespeare's water here represents irresponsible weakness.

Other Shakespearean resonances in the poem similarly evoke Shakespearean mistakes associated with water: At the end of part II, Eliot alludes to Ophelia's suicide and her fallacious belief that the water in which she drowned herself might bring her some respite. And in part III, allusions to *The Tempest* evoke Ferdinand's entranced delusions about the force of the water and what has really happened to the rulers of Naples and Milan in their sea journey.

Water is obviously a necessary element in *The Waste Land*, fundamentally important if one is to traverse and survive a dry, barren
landscape, but Shakespeare's water turns out to be a mirage: too
aesthetically attenuated, too unusable by the characters dazzled by
Shakespearean elegance, which derails the audience's attention to
the real stakes of the struggles.

In 1971, Eliot's second wife, Valerie, published a critical and facsimile edition presenting the drafts of the poem, adding a great deal
to our understanding of its genesis and development. We see
Pound's extensive and brilliant editing of a messy, uncertain manuscript, testimony to his crucial role as Eliot's midwife in the
poem's birth. A dedicatory epigraph thanks Pound as *'il miglior
fabbro'* — the better craftsman — and this crafting elucidates how a
murky, sometimes rambling set of observations (in the mode of
Eliot's first poetry collection) and dense, surreal conundrums (in
the mode of his second) became the clear, keen, vatic poesis of his
masterpiece.
  Pound added only two words to the poem: 'demobbed' (short
for 'demobilized' — sent home from the war) and 'demotic' ('common, popular, vulgar'): Mr. Eugenides, the Smyrna merchant,
unshaven, 'Asked me in demotic French' to a possibly sordid
luncheon and then a weekend at the Metropole. Mainly Pound
challenged and bolstered Eliot's voice; he queried and cut. He
edited the poem as if he were editing a film (cognizant that, in the
1920s, film was emerging as a bold and powerful new medium that
was perhaps uniquely qualified to capture the modern temperament): relegating large, ineffective passages to the cutting-room
floor; heightening a sense of sensory immediacy and direct visual
intensity; linking and juxtaposing scenes with quick, startling cuts.
He identified passages he found especially effective, such as the
second verse paragraph of part III, by scrawling 'echt' (meaning
veritable, real) in the margin, and worked to lift the entire manuscript up to that standard. Pound chided Eliot when he used the
word 'perhaps': 'Dam per'apsez,' he wrote in his idiosyncratic phonetic diction. He knew that this poem needed to resonate with
clear, crisp certainties, not equivocation. And again, when Eliot
wrote what is now line 251 ('Her brain allows one half-formed

thought to pass') in a less definitive mode ('Across her brain one half-formed thought may pass') Pound responded, 'make up yr. mind.' Pound nurtured the poem's clear, definitive voice, which he educed from a much more tentative draft—and Eliot's initial hesitations and uncertainties are completely understandable considering his tenuous mental and emotional condition during the first stage of composition.

Pound had also a strong sense of what the poem's style and meter should look like: its distinctive, hard, harsh sound and prosody emerged out of an earlier version that was more muddled and varied in style. 'Too loose,' he wrote by one passage, and 'rhyme drags it out to diffuseness' in another (both of which were cut: Eliot followed Pound's suggestions faithfully).

A few other interesting cuts and developments in the manuscript include an epigraph from Joseph Conrad's *Heart of Darkness*—the passage that conveys Kurtz's dying words—that was brilliantly apropos but, as Eliot and Pound presumably realized, too heavy-handed: superfluous. Indeed, we hear 'The horror! the horror!' in *The Waste Land* all the more clearly, and hauntingly, for the effacement of this epigraph. Part IV, 'Death by Water,' a tight, condensed, Imagist concentration of Phlebas the Phoenician's travail in the finished version, was at first a grueling, detailed sea narrative. Reading the manuscript, one appreciates that it was an important developmental effort for Eliot to have sketched out the entire fateful journey, but ultimately the keener effect was achieved when he jettisoned the long buildup and left only the quiet, slightly surreal, yet soothing denouement.

There was one other person besides Pound who helped to shape the poem: In the margin of the draft, Eliot's first wife, Vivien, wrote one phrase that appears in the final poem (slightly modified) as line 164: She placed an asterisk in the margin next to the passage about Lil and Albert and then wrote at the bottom of the page: 'What you get married for if you don't want to have children?' This line is central to the poem in so many ways: Barrenness and the danger of a society's failure or inability to perpetuate itself in a harsh, hostile world is a prominent theme. Line 164 suggests that perhaps this failure is volitional: Are people actively choosing not to have children? Is there something about modern marriage and sexual-emotional relationships that is so dysfunctionally noncommunicative as to forestall reproduction? (Think of all the miscues and retreats in 'Prufrock,' and 'Portrait of a Lady,' and 'Rhapsody on a Windy Night,' and the sexual torpor, or terror, or inertia, of the Sweeney poems and 'Hysteria' and 'Lune de Miel.')

Marriage and childbearing evoke the fusion (or here, the disjunction) between the social and the biological aspects of the most fundamental unit of society, the family. As Lil awaits her husband Albert's return from the military and cultural devastation of the Great War, her friends in a pub discuss her readiness (or unreadiness) for the reunion. She needs to make herself a bit smart—the years have taken a toll on her (and certainly they must have on him as well): Will they be attractive to each other? Or will they recoil from the horror of their appearances? Will they endure as a couple, or will the anticipated sexual disjunction propel him into the arms of another woman? Will they have more children, or would it kill her to go through childbirth again? Does she want children, or would she abort a future pregnancy as she did her previous one? Has her life made her infertile? How do one's personal, sexual, romantic drives weather the zeitgeist of the modern, postwar world? What and whom can one cling to? What can one expect for the future? All these questions resonate from Vivien's line.

I wonder if she even meant it to be a line in the poem, or rather, perhaps, just a biting aside to her husband? Possibly she meant the phrase not as a contribution to the text but a comment on it: an accusatory jab at Tom, who had gotten married and didn't seem to want children, leaving his poor unstable wife floundering in a world that must have looked to her very much like the milieu that infiltrates *The Waste Land*. And for an even further-flung conjecture: Perhaps not only didn't she mean for the line to be part of the poem, but Eliot actually realized this yet inserted it into the poem anyway, as his own self-abnegating, autobiographical *mea culpa* for his complicity in the perversely barren landscape he described.

Toward the end of the poem is a passage of surprising clarity and tranquillity: Eliot described lines 331–358 as 'the water-dripping song' and wrote to the novelist Ford Madox Ford about them:

'There are, *I* think, about 30 *good* lines in *The Waste Land*. Can you find them? The rest is ephemeral.' It may assist our overall comprehension of the poem's meaning, its moral, if we take Eliot at his word and try to determine what is good about this passage.

First of all, the language is less complex, and less unstable, than anywhere else in the poem. No foreign intertexts, no erudite allusions, no insane or bawdy interjections. The words are simple and calm. The rhetoric is, one might say, philosophical — logical — in a very concrete way: if–then constructions; clear assertions of reality and perception and presence/absence. The narrative expounds, in fairly graspable terms, a quest-object, and it is, simply enough, merely water: the force of life, the basic yet astounding compound that covers most of the earth. To paraphrase bluntly the tragedy of modern life, as Eliot formulates it in this passage: There is no water, so things are bad. If there were water, it would be better. But there is no water.

This seems ominous, unpromising. But there is also, in this passage, one glimmer of hope: 'If there were the sound of water only,' Eliot writes in line 353. The sound of water would obviously not be real water, but it might remind us of water, or inspire us to hold out hope until the water comes. And indeed the poem delivers on this hypothetical proposition just five lines later: 'Drip drop drip drop drop drop drop.' The line is probably the poem's simplest, perhaps its most banal, yet it is also its most fulfilling. Eliot and all the various and sundry cultural forces he summons throughout the poem cannot elsewhere complete or fulfill the gaps, the lacunae . . . but here, Eliot shows a kind of aesthetic power: If water cannot be had, then at least a poet with his tools (sounds!) can deliver an avatar of water. Lurking here is the suggestion, which one might not have expected given the cynicism about the potential of art elsewhere in the poem, that poetry can, in fact, endure and provide (or point the way toward) salvation.

There is a reiteration of this scene in lines 393–394: 'a flash of lightning. Then a damp gust / Bringing rain.' Again, there is no water, but there is the sound of water, the promise of water, the proximity of water, even the feel, damp, of water. The poem leaves readers, ultimately, in many ways still dry and barren at the end, but it does succeed in bringing us just about as close to water as possible without getting there—like Moses leading his people to within sight of the promised land. In this vein, I read the poem, finally, as guardedly optimistic: The poet has traversed the desert, and the burden of the poem is absorbing and conveying all the suffering and horror that accompanies this metaphorical journey through the wastes of civilization and culture and postwar Europe and the incoherent, overcharged, frighteningly hostile modern world. But there is a release, an achievement, a transcendence perhaps, a strength of having survived, that glimmers just beyond the poem's ending, or that might even manifest itself in the last three words, 'Shantih shantih shantih' ('The peace which passeth understanding'). At the end, we are left close to emergence.

The present collection ends with Eliot's masterpiece, and captures a vital aspect of Eliot's poetic, but it would be an oversight to neglect the second major phase of Eliot's life and career. In 1927 he converted to Anglo-Catholicism and published the devoutly meditative poem 'Ash-Wednesday,' which betokens a shift in his philosophy. The rest of his career was marked by a significant engagement in the consummately social medium of drama—a stark change from the solipsistic individualism of his poetry—and the poetic masterwork of this phase was *Four Quartets*, a poem of acceptance and forgiveness, moments of quiet peace and beauty, and (as it appeared during the throes of World War II) stoic endurance in the face of external devastation. He even wrote a collection of poems about cats (scored and produced by Andrew Lloyd Webber as a blockbuster musical, which, to the good fortune of the Eliot estate, has garnered probably more money in royalties than all the rest of his oeuvre). This more tolerant and accepting aesthetic of Eliot's later life is a counterpoint to the hostile, cynical tropes of his earlier work. I do not believe that Eliot meant for this later work to negate or repudiate the earlier, but rather to sit alongside it: The two parts of Eliot's career delineate two different approaches to the world, and it seems that Eliot believed both of them can be true. If one's inclination as a reader is to seek some ultimately affirmative insight, then one may extrapolate beyond the bleak defeatism that pervades Eliot's early poetry and see that, finally, he came to believe that Europe and culture and the human psyche will manage to endure.

Randy Malamud is Professor of English and Associate Chair of the department at Georgia State University in Atlanta. He received his Ph.D. from Columbia University and has taught modern literature at GSU since 1989. He is the author of three books about T. S. Eliot: *The Language of Modernism* (Ann Arbor: UMI Research Press, 1989), a study of linguistic and stylistic coherence in the work of Eliot, James Joyce, and Virginia Woolf; *T. S. Eliot's Drama: A Research and Production Sourcebook* (Westport, CT: Greenwood Press, 1992), a bibliographical reference work about Eliot's dramatic career; and *Where the Words Are Valid: T. S. Eliot's Communities of Drama* (Westport, CT: Greenwood Press, 1994), a critical study of Eliot's seven plays which argues that the social impetus of this work from his later career importantly complements the solipsistic strains of his earlier poetry. Dr. Malamud's most recent work deals with cultural studies of human-animal relationships: On this topic, he has written *Reading Zoos: Representations of Animals and Captivity* (New York: NYU Press, 1998) and *Poetic Animals and Animal Souls* (New York: Palgrave, 2003). His webpage, <http://www.gsu.edu/~wwweng/people/malamud.html>, lists contact information and links to articles he has written.

THE WASTE LAND
AND OTHER POEMS

PRUFROCK
AND OTHER OBSERVATIONS
1917

FOR JEAN VERDENAL, 1889–1915
MORT AUX DARDANELLES[1]

Or puoi quantitante
comprender dell' amor ch'a te mi scalda,
quando dismento nostra vanitate,
trattando l'ombre come cosa salda.[2]

Prufrock and Other Observations (1917)

The Love Song of J. Alfred Prufrock

S'io credessi che mia risposta fosse
a persona che mai tornasse al mondo,
questa fiamma staria senza piu scosse.
Ma per ciò che giammai di questo fondo
non tornò vivo alcun, s'i'odo il vero,
senza tema d'infamia ti rispondo.[1]

Let us go then, you and I,
When the evening is spread out against the sky
Like a patient etherised upon a table;
Let us go, through certain half-deserted streets,
The muttering retreats
Of restless nights in one-night cheap hotels
And sawdust restaurants with oyster-shells:
Streets that follow like a tedious argument
Of insidious intent
To lead you to an overwhelming question . . .
Oh, do not ask, 'What is it?'
Let us go and make our visit.

In the room the women come and go
Talking of Michelangelo.[2]

The yellow fog that rubs its back upon the window-
      panes,
The yellow smoke that rubs its muzzle on the
      window-panes
Licked its tongue into the corners of the evening,
Lingered upon the pools that stand in drains,
Let fall upon its back the soot that falls from
      chimneys,
Slipped by the terrace, made a sudden leap,
And seeing that it was a soft October night,
Curled once about the house, and fell asleep.

And indeed there will be time[3]
For the yellow smoke that slides along the street
Rubbing its back upon the window-panes;
There will be time, there will be time
To prepare a face to meet the faces that you meet;
There will be time to murder and create,
And time for all the works and days[4] of hands
That lift and drop a question on your plate;
Time for you and time for me,
And time yet for a hundred indecisions,
And for a hundred visions and revisions,
Before the taking of a toast and tea.

In the room the women come and go
Talking of Michelangelo.

And indeed there will be time
To wonder, 'Do I dare?' and, 'Do I dare?'
Time to turn back and descend the stair,
With a bald spot in the middle of my hair—
(They will say: 'How his hair is growing thin!')
My morning coat, my collar mounting firmly to
        the chin,
My necktie rich and modest, but asserted by a
        simple pin—
(They will say: 'But how his arms and legs are
        thin!')
Do I dare
Disturb the universe?
In a minute there is time
For decisions and revisions which a minute will
        reverse.

For I have known them all already, known them
        all—
Have known the evenings, mornings, afternoons,
I have measured out my life with coffee spoons;
I know the voices dying with a dying fall[5]

Beneath the music from a farther room.
   So how should I presume?

And I have known the eyes already, known them
   all—
The eyes that fix you in a formulated phrase,
And when I am formulated, sprawling on a pin,
When I am pinned and wriggling on the wall,
Then how should I begin
To spit out all the butt-ends of my days and ways?
   And how should I presume?

And I have known the arms already, known them
   all—
Arms that are braceleted and white and bare
(But in the lamplight, downed with light brown
   hair!)
Is it perfume from a dress
That makes me so digress?
Arms that lie along a table, or wrap about a shawl.
   And should I then presume?
   And how should I begin?

. . . . . .

Shall I say, I have gone at dusk through narrow
   streets
And watched the smoke that rises from the pipes
Of lonely men in shirt-sleeves, leaning out of
   windows? . . .

I should have been a pair of ragged claws
Scuttling across the floors of silent seas.

. . . . . .

And the afternoon, the evening, sleeps so peace-
   fully!
Smoothed by long fingers,
Asleep . . . tired . . . or it malingers,

Stretched on the floor, here beside you and me.
Should I, after tea and cakes and ices,
Have the strength to force the moment to its crisis?
But though I have wept and fasted, wept and
    prayed,
Though I have seen my head (grown slightly bald)
    brought in upon a platter,[6]
I am no prophet—and here's no great matter;
I have seen the moment of my greatness flicker,
And I have seen the eternal Footman hold my
    coat, and snicker,
And in short, I was afraid.

And would it have been worth it, after all,
After the cups, the marmalade, the tea,
Among the porcelain, among some talk of you and
    me,
Would it have been worth while,
To have bitten off the matter with a smile,
To have squeezed the universe into a ball[7]
To roll it toward some overwhelming question,
To say: 'I am Lazarus, come from the dead,[8]
Come back to tell you all, I shall tell you all'—
If one, settling a pillow by her head,
    Should say: 'That is not what I meant at all.
    That is not it, at all.'

And would it have been worth it, after all,
Would it have been worth while,
After the sunsets and the dooryards and the
    sprinkled streets,
After the novels, after the teacups, after the skirts
    that trail along the floor—
And this, and so much more?—
It is impossible to say just what I mean!
But as if a magic lantern[9] threw the nerves in
    patterns on a screen:
Would it have been worth while

If one, settling a pillow or throwing off a shawl,
And turning toward the window, should say:
    'That is not it at all,
    That is not what I meant, at all.'

    .   .   .   .   .

No! I am not Prince Hamlet,[10] nor was meant to
    be;
Am an attendant lord, one that will do
To swell a progress, start a scene or two,
Advise the prince; no doubt, an easy tool,
Deferential, glad to be of use,
Politic, cautious, and meticulous;
Full of high sentence, but a bit obtuse;
At times, indeed, almost ridiculous—
Almost, at times, the Fool.[11]

I grow old . . . I grow old . . .
I shall wear the bottoms of my trousers rolled.

Shall I part my hair behind? Do I dare to eat a
    peach?
I shall wear white flannel trousers, and walk upon
    the beach.
I have heard the mermaids singing,[12] each to each.

I do not think that they will sing to me.

I have seen them riding seaward on the waves
Combing the white hair of the waves blown back
When the wind blows the water white and black.

We have lingered in the chambers of the sea
By sea-girls wreathed with seaweed red and brown
Till human voices wake us, and we drown.

Portrait of a Lady

Thou hast committed—
Fornication: but that was in another country,
And besides, the wench is dead.

THE JEW OF MALTA.[1]

I

Among the smoke and fog of a December
        afternoon
You have the scene arrange itself—as it will seem
        to do—
With 'I have saved this afternoon for you';
And four wax candles in the darkened room,
Four rings of light upon the ceiling overhead,
An atmosphere of Juliet's tomb[2]
Prepared for all the things to be said, or left unsaid.
We have been, let us say, to hear the latest Pole
Transmit the Preludes,[3] through his hair and
        finger-tips.
'So intimate, this Chopin, that I think his soul
Should be resurrected only among friends
Some two or three, who will not touch the bloom
That is rubbed and questioned in the concert
        room.'
—And so the conversation slips
Among velleities[4] and carefully caught regrets
Through attenuated tones of violins
Mingled with remote cornets
And begins.
'You do not know how much they mean to me, my
        friends,
And how, how rare and strange it is, to find
In a life composed so much, so much of odds and
        ends,

(For indeed I do not love it . . . you knew? you are
    not blind!
How keen you are!)
To find a friend who has these qualities,
Who has, and gives
Those qualities upon which friendship lives.
How much it means that I say this to you—
Without these friendships—life, what *cauchemar!*'[5]

Among the windings of the violins
And the ariettes[6]
Of cracked cornets
Inside my brain a dull tom-tom begins
Absurdly hammering a prelude of its own,
Capricious monotone
That is at least one definite 'false note.'
—Let us take the air, in a tobacco trance,
Admire the monuments,
Discuss the late events,
Correct our watches by the public clocks.
Then sit for half an hour and drink our bocks.[7]

II

Now that lilacs are in bloom
She has a bowl of lilacs in her room
And twists one in her fingers while she talks.
'Ah, my friend, you do not know, you do not know
What life is, you who hold it in your hands';
(Slowly twisting the lilac stalks)
'You let it flow from you, you let it flow,
And youth is cruel, and has no remorse
And smiles at situations which it cannot see.'
I smile, of course,
And go on drinking tea.
'Yet with these April sunsets, that somehow recall
My buried life, and Paris in the Spring,
I feel immeasurably at peace, and find the world
To be wonderful and youthful, after all.'

The voice returns like the insistent out-of-tune
Of a broken violin on an August afternoon:
'I am always sure that you understand
My feelings, always sure that you feel,
Sure that across the gulf you reach your hand.

You are invulnerable, you have no Achilles' heel.
You will go on, and when you have prevailed
You can say: at this point many a one has failed.
But what have I, but what have I, my friend,
To give you, what can you receive from me?
Only the friendship and the sympathy
Of one about to reach her journey's end.

I shall sit here, serving tea to friends. . . .'

I take my hat: how can I make a cowardly amends
For what she has said to me?
You will see me any morning in the park
Reading the comics and the sporting page.
Particularly I remark
An English countess goes upon the stage.
A Greek was murdered at a Polish dance,
Another bank defaulter has confessed.
I keep my countenance,
I remain self-possessed
Except when a street piano, mechanical and tired
Reiterates some worn-out common song
With the smell of hyacinths across the garden
Recalling things that other people have desired.
Are these ideas right or wrong?

III

The October night comes down; returning as
        before
Except for a slight sensation of being ill at ease
I mount the stairs and turn the handle of the door

And feel as if I had mounted on my hands and
    knees.
'And so you are going abroad; and when do you
    return?
But that's a useless question.
You hardly know when you are coming back,
You will find so much to learn.'
My smile falls heavily among the bric-à-brac.

'Perhaps you can write to me.'
My self-possession flares up for a second;
This is as I had reckoned.
'I have been wondering frequently of late
(But our beginnings never know our ends!)
Why we have not developed into friends.'
I feel like one who smiles, and turning shall
    remark
Suddenly, his expression in a glass.
My self-possession gutters; we are really in the dark.

'For everybody said so, all our friends,[8]
They all were sure our feelings would relate
So closely! I myself can hardly understand.
We must leave it now to fate.
You will write, at any rate.
Perhaps it is not too late.
I shall sit here, serving tea to friends.'

And I must borrow every changing shape
To find expression . . . dance, dance
Like a dancing bear,
Cry like a parrot, chatter like an ape.
Let us take the air, in a tobacco trance—

Well! and what if she should die some afternoon,
Afternoon grey and smoky, evening yellow and
    rose;

Should die and leave me sitting pen in hand
With the smoke coming down above the
　　housetops;
Doubtful, for a while
Not knowing what to feel or if I understand
Or whether wise or foolish, tardy or too soon . . .
Would she not have the advantage, after all?
This music is successful with a 'dying fall'9
Now that we talk of dying—
And should I have the right to smile?

Preludes

I

The winter evening settles down
With smell of steaks in passageways.
Six o'clock.
The burnt-out ends of smoky days.
And now a gusty shower wraps
The grimy scraps
Of withered leaves about your feet
And newspapers from vacant lots;
The showers beat
On broken blinds and chimney-pots,
And at the corner of the street
A lonely cab-horse steams and stamps.

And then the lighting of the lamps.

II

The morning comes to consciousness
Of faint stale smells of beer
From the sawdust-trampled street
With all its muddy feet that press
To early coffee-stands.

With the other masquerades
That time resumes,
One thinks of all the hands
That are raising dingy shades
In a thousand furnished rooms.

III

You tossed a blanket from the bed,
You lay upon your back, and waited;
You dozed, and watched the night revealing
The thousand sordid images

Of which your soul was constituted;
They flickered against the ceiling.
And when all the world came back
And the light crept up between the shutters
And you heard the sparrows in the gutters,
You had such a vision of the street
As the street hardly understands;
Sitting along the bed's edge, where
You curled the papers from your hair,
Or clasped the yellow soles of feet
In the palms of both soiled hands.

IV

His soul stretched tight across the skies
That fade behind a city block,
Or trampled by insistent feet
At four and five and six o'clock;
And short square fingers stuffing pipes,
And evening newspapers, and eyes
Assured of certain certainties,
The conscience of a blackened street
Impatient to assume the world.

I am moved by fancies that are curled
Around these images, and cling:
The notion of some infinitely gentle
Infinitely suffering thing.

Wipe your hand across your mouth, and laugh;
The worlds revolve like ancient women
Gathering fuel in vacant lots.

Rhapsody on a Windy Night

Twelve o'clock.
Along the reaches of the street
Held in a lunar synthesis,[1]
Whispering lunar incantations
Dissolve the floors of memory[2]
And all its clear relations
Its divisions and precisions.
Every street lamp that I pass
Beats like a fatalistic drum,
And through the spaces of the dark
Midnight shakes the memory
As a madman shakes a dead geranium.

Half-past one,
The street-lamp sputtered,
The street-lamp muttered,
The street-lamp said, 'Regard that woman[3]
Who hesitates toward you in the light of the door
Which opens on her like a grin.
You see the border of her dress
Is torn and stained with sand,
And you see the corner of her eye
Twists like a crooked pin.'

The memory throws up high and dry
A crowd of twisted things;
A twisted branch upon the beach
Eaten smooth, and polished
As if the world gave up
The secret of its skeleton,
Stiff and white.
A broken spring in a factory yard,
Rust that clings to the form that the strength has left
Hard and curled and ready to snap.

Half-past two,
The street-lamp said,
'Remark the cat which flattens itself in the gutter,
Slips out its tongue
And devours a morsel of rancid butter.'
So the hand of the child, automatic,
Slipped out and pocketed a toy that was running
    along the quay.
I could see nothing behind that child's eye.
I have seen eyes in the street
Trying to peer through lighted shutters,
And a crab one afternoon in a pool,
An old crab with barnacles on his back,
Gripped the end of a stick which I held him.

Half-past three,
The lamp sputtered,
The lamp muttered in the dark.
The lamp hummed:
'Regard the moon,
La lune ne garde aucune rancune,
She winks a feeble eye,
She smiles into corners.
She smooths the hair of the grass.
The moon has lost her memory.
A washed-out smallpox cracks her face,
Her hand twists a paper rose,
That smells of dust and eau de Cologne,
She is alone
With all the old nocturnal smells
That cross and cross across her brain.'
The reminiscence comes
Of sunless dry geraniums
And dust in crevices,
Smells of chestnuts in the streets,
And female smells in shuttered rooms,
And cigarettes in corridors
And cocktail smells in bars.

The lamp said,
'Four o'clock,
Here is the number on the door.
Memory!
You have the key,
The little lamp spreads a ring on the stair.
Mount.
The bed is open; the tooth-brush hangs on the
    wall,
Put your shoes at the door, sleep, prepare for life.'

The last twist of the knife.

Morning at the Window

They are rattling breakfast plates in basement
    kitchens,
And along the trampled edges of the street
I am aware of the damp souls of housemaids
Sprouting despondently at area gates.

The brown waves of fog toss up to me
Twisted faces from the bottom of the street,
And tear from a passer-by with muddy skirts
An aimless smile that hovers in the air
And vanishes along the level of the roofs.

The *Boston Evening Transcript*

The readers of the *Boston Evening Transcript*
Sway in the wind like a field of ripe corn.

When evening quickens faintly in the street,
Wakening the appetites of life in some
And to others bringing the *Boston Evening
Transcript*,
I mount the steps and ring the bell, turning
Wearily, as one would turn to nod good-bye to
La Rochefoucauld,[1]
If the street were time and he at the end of the
street,
And I say, 'Cousin Harriet, here is the *Boston
Evening Transcript*.'

Aunt Helen

Miss Helen Slingsby was my maiden aunt,
And lived in a small house near a fashionable
    square
Cared for by servants to the number of four.
Now when she died there was silence in heaven
And silence at her end of the street.
The shutters were drawn and the undertaker wiped
    his feet—
He was aware that this sort of thing had occurred
    before.
The dogs were handsomely provided for,
But shortly afterwards the parrot died too.
The Dresden clock continued ticking on the
    mantelpiece,
And the footman sat upon the dining-table
Holding the second housemaid on his knees—
Who had always been so careful while her mistress
    lived.

Cousin Nancy

Miss Nancy Ellicott
Strode across the hills and broke them,
Rode across the hills and broke them—
The barren New England hills—
Riding to hounds
Over the cow-pasture.

Miss Nancy Ellicott smoked
And danced all the modern dances;
And her aunts were not quite sure how they felt
    about it,
But they knew that it was modern.

Upon the glazen shelves kept watch
Matthew and Waldo,[1] guardians of the faith,
The army of unalterable law.

Mr. Apollinax

Ω τῆς καινότητος. Ἡράκλειζ, τῆς παραδοξολογίας.
εὐμήχανος ἄνθρωπος.

LUCIAN.[1]

When Mr. Apollinax[2] visited the United States
His laughter tinkled among the teacups.
I thought of Fragilion, that shy figure among the
    birch-trees,
And of Priapus[3] in the shrubbery
Gaping at the lady in the swing.
In the palace of Mrs. Phlaccus, at Professor
    Channing-Cheetah's
He laughed like an irresponsible fœtus.
His laughter was submarine and profound
Like the old man of the sea's
Hidden under coral islands
Where worried bodies of drowned men drift down
    in the green silence,
Dropping from fingers of surf.

I looked for the head of Mr. Apollinax rolling
    under a chair.
Or grinning over a screen
With seaweed in its hair.
I heard the beat of centaur's hoofs over the hard
    turf
As his dry and passionate talk devoured the
    afternoon.
'He is a charming man' — 'But after all what did he
    mean?' —
'His pointed ears. . . . He must be unbalanced.' —
'There was something he said that I might have
    challenged.'

28

Of dowager Mrs. Phlaccus, and Professor and
    Mrs. Cheetah
I remember a slice of lemon, and a bitten
    macaroon.

Hysteria

As she laughed I was aware of becoming involved
in her laughter and being part of it, until her teeth
were only accidental stars with a talent for
squad-drill. I was drawn in by short gasps, inhaled
at each momentary recovery, lost finally in the
dark caverns of her throat, bruised by the ripple of
unseen muscles. An elderly waiter with trembling
hands was hurriedly spreading a pink and white
checked cloth over the rusty green iron table,
saying: 'If the lady and gentleman wish to take
their tea in the garden, if the lady and gentleman
wish to take their tea in the garden . . .' I decided
that if the shaking of her breasts could be stopped,
some of the fragments of the afternoon might be
collected, and I concentrated my attention with
careful subtlety to this end.

Conversation Galante

I observe: 'Our sentimental friend the moon!
Or possibly (fantastic, I confess)
It may be Prester John's[1] balloon
Or an old battered lantern hung aloft
To light poor travellers to their distress.'
    She then: 'How you digress!'

And I then: 'Someone frames upon the keys
That exquisite nocturne, with which we explain
The night and moonshine; music which we seize
To body forth our own vacuity.'
    She then: 'Does this refer to me?'
    'Oh no, it is I who am inane.'

'You, madam, are the eternal humorist,
The eternal enemy of the absolute,
Giving our vagrant moods the slightest twist!
With your air indifferent and imperious
At a stroke our mad poetics to confute—'
    And—'Are we then so serious?'

La Figlia che Piange[1]

O quam te memorem virgo . . .[2]

Stand on the highest pavement of the stair—
Lean on a garden urn—
Weave, weave the sunlight in your hair—
Clasp your flowers to you with a pained surprise—
Fling them to the ground and turn
With a fugitive resentment in your eyes:
But weave, weave the sunlight in your hair.

So I would have had him leave,
So I would have had her stand and grieve,
So he would have left
As the soul leaves the body torn and bruised,
As the mind deserts the body it has used.
I should find
Some way incomparably light and deft,
Some way we both should understand,
Simple and faithless as a smile and shake of the
      hand.

She turned away, but with the autumn weather
Compelled my imagination many days,
Many days and many hours:
Her hair over her arms and her arms full of
      flowers.
And I wonder how they should have been together!
I should have lost a gesture and a pose.
Sometimes these cogitations still amaze
The troubled midnight and the noon's repose.

POEMS 1920

Poems 1920

Gerontion[1]

Thou hast nor youth nor age
But as it were an after dinner sleep
Dreaming of both.[2]

Here I am, an old man in a dry month,
Being read to by a boy, waiting for rain.
I was neither at the hot gates
Nor fought in the warm rain
Nor knee deep in the salt marsh, heaving a
    cutlass,
Bitten by flies, fought.
My house is a decayed house,
And the Jew squats on the window sill, the owner,
Spawned in some estaminet[3] of Antwerp,
Blistered in Brussels, patched and peeled in
    London.
The goat coughs at night in the field overhead;
Rocks, moss, stonecrop, iron, merds.
The woman keeps the kitchen, makes tea,
Sneezes at evening, poking the peevish gutter.
                      I an old man,
A dull head among windy spaces.

Signs are taken for wonders. 'We would see a sign!'[4]
The word within a word, unable to speak a word,
Swaddled with darkness. In the juvescence of the
    year
Came Christ the tiger

In depraved May, dogwood and chestnut, flowering
    judas,[5]
To be eaten, to be divided, to be drunk
Among whispers; by Mr. Silvero

With caressing hands, at Limoges[6]
Who walked all night in the next room;

By Hakagawa, bowing among the Titians;
By Madame de Tornquist, in the dark room
Shifting the candles; Fräulein von Kulp[7]
Who turned in the hall, one hand on the door.
    Vacant shuttles
Weave the wind. I have no ghosts,
An old man in a draughty house
Under a windy knob.

After such knowledge, what forgiveness? Think
    now
History has many cunning passages, contrived
    corridors[8]
And issues, deceives with whispering ambitions,
Guides us by vanities. Think now
She gives when our attention is distracted
And what she gives, gives with such supple
    confusions
That the giving famishes the craving. Gives too late
What's not believed in, or if still believed,
In memory only, reconsidered passion. Gives too
    soon
Into weak hands,[9] what's thought can be dispensed
    with
Till the refusal propagates a fear. Think
Neither fear nor courage saves us. Unnatural vices
Are fathered by our heroism. Virtues
Are forced upon us by our impudent crimes.
These tears are shaken from the wrath-bearing
    tree.[10]

The tiger springs in the new year. Us he devours.
    Think at last
We have not reached conclusion, when I
Stiffen in a rented house. Think at last

I have not made this show purposelessly
And it is not by any concitation
Of the backward devils.
I would meet you upon this honestly.
I that was near your heart was removed therefrom
To lose beauty in terror, terror in inquisition.
I have lost my passion: why should I need to
keep it
Since what is kept must be adulterated?
I have lost my sight, smell, hearing, taste and
touch:
How should I use them for your closer contact?

These with a thousand small deliberations
Protract the profit of their chilled delirium,
Excite the membrane, when the sense has cooled,
With pungent sauces, multiply variety
In a wilderness of mirrors. What will the spider do,
Suspend its operations, will the weevil
Delay? De Bailhache, Fresca, Mrs. Cammel,[11]
whirled
Beyond the circuit of the shuddering Bear[12]
In fractured atoms. Gull against the wind, in the
windy straits
Of Belle Isle,[13] or running on the Horn.[14]
White feathers in the snow, the Gulf claims,
And an old man driven by the Trades[15]
To a sleepy corner.

                    Tenants of the house,
Thoughts of a dry brain in a dry season.

Burbank with a Baedeker:[1]
Bleistein with a Cigar

Tra-la-la-la-la-la-laire—nil nisi divinum stabile est; caetera fumus—the gondola stopped, the old palace was there, how charming its grey and pink—goats and monkeys, with such hair too!—so the countess passed on until she came through the little park, where Niobe presented her with a cabinet, and so departed.[2]

Burbank crossed a little bridge
    Descending at a small hotel;
Princess Volupine[3] arrived,
    They were together, and he fell.[4]

Defunctive music under sea
    Passed seaward with the passing bell
Slowly: the God Hercules[5]
    Had left him, that had loved him well.

The horses, under the axletree
    Beat up the dawn from Istria[6]
With even feet. Her shuttered barge
    Burned on the water all the day.

But this or such was Bleistein's way:
    A saggy bending of the knees
And elbows, with the palms turned out,
    Chicago Semite Viennese.

A lustreless protrusive eye
    Stares from the protozoic slime
At a perspective of Canaletto.[7]
    The smoky candle end of time

Declines. On the Rialto[8] once.
    The rats are underneath the piles.

The Jew is underneath the lot.
    Money in furs. The boatman smiles,

Princess Volupine extends
    A meagre, blue-nailed, phthisic hand
To climb the waterstair. Lights, lights,
    She entertains Sir Ferdinand

Klein. Who clipped the lion's wings[9]
    And flea'd his rump and pared his claws?
Thought Burbank, meditating on
    Time's ruins, and the seven laws.

Sweeney Erect

And the trees about me,
Let them be dry and leafless; let the rocks
Groan with continual surges; and behind me
Make all a desolation. Look, look, wenches![1]

Paint me a cavernous waste shore
    Cast in the unstilled Cyclades,[2]
Paint me the bold anfractuous rocks
    Faced by the snarled and yelping seas.

Display me Aeolus[3] above
    Reviewing the insurgent gales
Which tangle Ariadne's[4] hair
    And swell with haste the perjured sails.

Morning stirs the feet and hands
    (Nausicaa[5] and Polypheme[6]).
Gesture of orang-outang
    Rises from the sheets in steam.

This withered root of knots of hair
    Slitted below and gashed with eyes,
This oval O cropped out with teeth:
    The sickle motion from the thighs

Jackknifes upward at the knees
    Then straightens out from heel to hip
Pushing the framework of the bed
    And clawing at the pillow slip.

Sweeney addressed full length to shave
    Broadbottomed, pink from nape to base,
Knows the female temperament
    And wipes the suds around his face.

(The lengthened shadow of a man
    Is history, said Emerson[7]
Who had not seen the silhouette
    Of Sweeney straddled in the sun.)

Tests the razor on his leg
    Waiting until the shriek subsides.
The epileptic on the bed
    Curves backward, clutching at her sides.

The ladies of the corridor
    Find themselves involved, disgraced,
Call witness to their principles
    And deprecate the lack of taste

Observing that hysteria
    Might easily be misunderstood;
Mrs. Turner intimates
    It does the house no sort of good.

But Doris, towelled from the bath,
    Enters padding on broad feet,
Bringing sal volatile
    And a glass of brandy neat.

A Cooking Egg[1]

En l'an trentiesme de mon aage
Que toutes mes hontes j'ay beues . . .[2]

Pipit sate upright in her chair
    Some distance from where I was sitting;
Views of the Oxford Colleges
    Lay on the table, with the knitting.

Daguerreotypes and silhouettes,
    Her grandfather and great great aunts,
Supported on the mantelpiece
    An *Invitation to the Dance.*[3]

.   .   .   .   .

I shall not want Honour in Heaven
    For I shall meet Sir Philip Sidney[4]
And have talk with Coriolanus[5]
    And other heroes of that kidney.

I shall not want Capital in Heaven
    For I shall meet Sir Alfred Mond.[6]
We two shall lie together, lapt
    In a five per cent. Exchequer Bond.

I shall not want Society in Heaven,
    Lucretia Borgia[7] shall be my Bride;
Her anecdotes will be more amusing
    Than Pipit's experience could provide.

I shall not want Pipit in Heaven:
    Madame Blavatsky[8] will instruct me
In the Seven Sacred Trances;[9]
    Piccarda de Donati[10] will conduct me.

.   .   .   .   .

But where is the penny world[11] I bought
    To eat with Pipit behind the screen?
The red-eyed scavengers are creeping
    From Kentish Town and Golder's Green;[12]

Where are the eagles and the trumpets?

    Buried beneath some snow-deep Alps.
Over buttered scones and crumpets
    Weeping, weeping multitudes
Droop in a hundred A.B.C.'s.[13]

Le Directeur[1]

Malheur à la malheureuse Tamise
Qui coule si près du Spectateur.[2]
Le directeur
Conservateur
Du Spectateur
Empeste la brise.
Les actionnaires
Réactionnaires
Du Spectateur
Conservateur
Bras dessus bras dessous
Font des tours
A pas de loup.
Dans un égout
Une petite fille
En guenilles
Camarde
Regarde
Le directeur
Du Spectateur
Conservateur
Et crève d'amour.

Mélange Adultère de Tout[1]

En Amérique, professeur;
En Angleterre, journaliste;
C'est à grands pas et en sueur
Que vous suivrez à peine ma piste.
En Yorkshire, conférencier;
A Londres, un peu banquier,
Vous me paierez bien la tête.
C'est à Paris que je me coiffe
Casque noir de jemenfoutiste.
En Allemagne, philosophe
Surexcité par Emporheben
Au grand air de Bergsteigleben;
J'erre toujours de-ci de-là
A divers coups de tra là là
De Damas jusqu'à Omaha.
Je célébrai mon jour de fête
Dans une oasis d'Afrique
Vêtu d'une peau de girafe.

On montrera mon cénotaphe
Aux côtes brûlantes de Mozambique.

Lune de Miel[1]

Ils ont vu les Pays-Bas, ils rentrent à Terre Haute;
Mais une nuit d'été, les voici à Ravenne,
A l'aise entre deux draps, chez deux centaines de
    punaises;
La sueur aestivale, et une forte odeur de chienne.
Ils restent sur le dos écartant les genoux
De quatre jambes molles tout gonflées de
    morsures.
On relève le drap pour mieux égratigner.
Moins d'une lieue d'ici est Saint Apollinaire
En Classe, basilique connue des amateurs
De chapitaux d'acanthe que tournoie le vent.

Ils vont prendre le train de huit heures
Prolonger leurs misères de Padoue à Milan
Où se trouvent la Cène, et un restaurant pas cher.
Lui pense aux pourboires, et rédige son bilan.
Ils auront vu la Suisse et traversé la France.
Et Saint Apollinaire, raide et ascétique,
Vieille usine désaffectée de Dieu, tient encore
Dans ses pierres écroulantes la forme précise de
    Byzance.

The Hippopotamus[1]

Similiter et omnes revereantur Diaconos, ut mandatum Jesu Christi; et Episcopum, ut Jesum Christum, existentem filium Patris; Presbyteros autem, ut concilium Dei et conjunctionem Apostolorum. Sine his Ecclesia non vocatur; de quibus suadeo vos sic habeo.

S. Ignatii Ad Trallianos.[2]

And when this epistle is read among you, cause that it be read also in the church of the Laodiceans.[3]

The broad-backed hippopotamus
Rests on his belly in the mud;
Although he seems so firm to us
He is merely flesh and blood.

Flesh and blood is weak and frail,
Susceptible to nervous shock;
While the True Church can never fail
For it is based upon a rock.[4]

The hippo's feeble steps may err
In compassing material ends,
While the True Church need never stir
To gather in its dividends.

The 'potamus can never reach
The mango on the mango-tree;
But fruits of pomegranate and peach
Refresh the Church from over sea.

At mating time the hippo's voice
Betrays inflexions hoarse and odd,
But every week we hear rejoice
The Church, at being one with God.

The hippopotamus's day
Is passed in sleep; at night he hunts;
God works in a mysterious way—
The Church can sleep and feed at once.

I saw the 'potamus take wing
Ascending from the damp savannas,
And quiring⁵ angels round him sing
The praise of God, in loud hosannas.

Blood of the Lamb shall wash him clean
And him shall heavenly arms enfold,
Among the saints he shall be seen
Performing on a harp of gold.

He shall be washed as white as snow,
By all the martyr'd virgins kist,
While the True Church remains below
Wrapt in the old miasmal mist.

Dans le Restaurant[1]

Le garçon délabré qui n'a rien à faire
Que de se gratter les doigts et se pencher sur mon
    épaule:
    'Dans mon pays il fera temps pluvieux,
    Du vent, du grand soleil, et de la pluie;
    C'est ce qu'on appelle le jour de lessive des
        gueux.'
(Bavard, baveux, à la croupe arrondie,
Je te prie, au moins, ne bave pas dans la soupe.)
    'Les saules trempés, et des bourgeons sur les
        ronces—
    C'est là, dans une averse, qu'on s'abrite.
J'avais sept ans, elle était plus petite.
    Elle était toute mouillée, je lui ai donné des
        primevères.'
Les taches de son gilet montent au chiffre de
    trente-huit.
    'Je la chatouillais, pour la faire rire.
    J'éprouvais un instant de puissance et de délire.'

    Mais alors, vieux lubrique, à cet âge . . .
'Monsieur, le fait est dur.
    Il est venu, nous peloter, un gros chien;
    Moi j'avais peur, je l'ai quittée à mi-chemin.
    C'est dommage.'
        Mais alors, tu as ton vautour!
Va t'en te décrotter les rides du visage;
Tiens, ma fourchette, décrasse-toi le crâne.
De quel droit payes-tu des expériences comme moi?
Tiens, voilà dix sous, pour la salle-de-bains.

Phlébas, le Phénicien, pendant quinze jours noyé,
Oubliait les cris des mouettes et la houle de
    Cornouaille,

Et les profits et les pertes, et la cargaison d'étain:
Un courant de sous-mer l'emporta très loin,
Le repassant aux étapes de sa vie antérieure.
Figurez-vous donc, c'était un sort pénible;
Cependant, ce fut jadis un bel homme, de haute
    taille.

Whispers of Immortality

Webster[1] was much possessed by death
And saw the skull beneath the skin;
And breastless creatures under ground
Leaned backward with a lipless grin.

Daffodil bulbs instead of balls
Stared from the sockets of the eyes!
He knew that thought clings round dead limbs
Tightening its lusts and luxuries.

Donne,[2] I suppose, was such another
Who found no substitute for sense,
To seize and clutch and penetrate;
Expert beyond experience,

He knew the anguish of the marrow
The ague of the skeleton;
No contact possible to flesh
Allayed the fever of the bone.

       · · · · ·

Grishkin[3] is nice: her Russian eye
Is underlined for emphasis;
Uncorseted, her friendly bust
Gives promise of pneumatic bliss.

The couched Brazilian jaguar
Compels the scampering marmoset
With subtle effluence of cat;
Grishkin has a maisonette;

The sleek Brazilian jaguar
Does not in its arboreal gloom

Distil so rank a feline smell
As Grishkin in a drawing-room.

And even the Abstract Entities[4]
Circumambulate her charm;
But our lot crawls between dry ribs
To keep our metaphysics warm.

Mr. Eliot's Sunday Morning Service

Look, look, master, here comes two religious caterpillars.

THE JEW OF MALTA.[1]

Polyphiloprogenitive[2]
The sapient sutlers[3] of the Lord
Drift across the window-panes.
In the beginning was the Word.

In the beginning was the Word.
Superfetation[4] of $\tau\grave{o}$ $\overset{\prime}{\varepsilon}\nu$,[5]
And at the mensual[6] turn of time
Produced enervate Origen.[7]

A painter of the Umbrian school[8]
Designed upon a gesso ground[9]
The nimbus[10] of the Baptized God.
The wilderness is cracked and browned

But through the water pale and thin
Still shine the unoffending feet
And there above the painter set
The Father and the Paraclete.[11]

. . . . .

The sable presbyters[12] approach
The avenue of penitence;
The young are red and pustular
Clutching piaculative pence.[13]

Under the penitential gates
Sustained by staring Seraphim[14]
Where the souls of the devout
Burn invisible and dim.

Along the garden-wall the bees
With hairy bellies pass between
The staminate and pistillate,[15]
Blest office of the epicene.[16]

Sweeney shifts from ham to ham
Stirring the water in his bath.
The masters of the subtle schools
Are controversial, polymath.[17]

Sweeney Among the Nightingales[1]

ὤμοι, πέπληγμαι καιρίαν πληγὴν ἔσω.[2]

Apeneck Sweeney spreads his knees
Letting his arms hang down to laugh,
The zebra stripes along his jaw
Swelling to maculate[3] giraffe.

The circles of the stormy moon
Slide westward toward the River Plate,[4]
Death and the Raven drift above
And Sweeney guards the hornèd gate.

Gloomy Orion and the Dog[5]
Are veiled; and hushed the shrunken seas;
The person in the Spanish cape
Tries to sit on Sweeney's knees

Slips and pulls the table cloth
Overturns a coffee-cup,
Reorganized upon the floor
She yawns and draws a stocking up;

The silent man in mocha brown
Sprawls at the window-sill and gapes;
The waiter brings in oranges
Bananas figs and hothouse grapes;

The silent vertebrate in brown
Contracts and concentrates, withdraws;
Rachel *née* Rabinovitch
Tears at the grapes with murderous paws;[6]

She and the lady in the cape
Are suspect, thought to be in league;

Therefore the man with heavy eyes
Declines the gambit, shows fatigue,

Leaves the room and reappears
Outside the window, leaning in,
Branches of wistaria
Circumscribe a golden grin;

The host with someone indistinct
Converses at the door apart,
The nightingales are singing near
The Convent of the Sacred Heart,[7]

And sang within the bloody wood
When Agamemnon[8] cried aloud,
And let their liquid siftings fall
To stain the stiff dishonoured shroud.

THE WASTE LAND

1922

'Nam Sibyllam quidem Cumis ego ipse oculis meis vidi in ampulla pendere, et cum illi pueri dicerent: Σίβυλλα τί θέλεις; respondebat illa: ἀποθανεῖν θέλω.'[1]

For Ezra Pound
il miglior fabbro.[2]

The Waste Land (1922)

I. *The Burial of the Dead*[1]

April is the cruellest month,[2] breeding
Lilacs out of the dead land, mixing
Memory and desire, stirring
Dull roots with spring rain.
Winter kept us warm, covering
Earth in forgetful snow, feeding
A little life with dried tubers.
Summer surprised us, coming over the
    Starnbergersee[3]
With a shower of rain; we stopped in the
    colonnade,
And went on in sunlight, into the Hofgarten,[4]   10
And drank coffee, and talked for an hour.
Bin gar keine Russin, stamm' aus Litauen, echt
    deutsch.[5]
And when we were children, staying at the
    arch-duke's,
My cousin's, he took me out on a sled,
And I was frightened. He said, Marie,
Marie, hold on tight. And down we went.
In the mountains, there you feel free.
I read, much of the night, and go south in the
    winter.

What are the roots that clutch, what branches grow
Out of this stony rubbish? Son of man,[6]   20
You cannot say, or guess, for you know only
A heap of broken images, where the sun beats,
And the dead tree gives no shelter, the cricket no
    relief,[7]
And the dry stone no sound of water. Only
There is shadow under this red rock,
(Come in under the shadow of this red rock),
And I will show you something different from either

Your shadow at morning striding behind you
Or your shadow at evening rising to meet you;
I will show you fear in a handful of dust.
> *Frisch weht der Wind*
> *Der Heimat zu*
> *Mein Irisch Kind,*
> *Wo weilest du?*[8]
'You gave me hyacinths first a year ago;
'They called me the hyacinth girl.'
—Yet when we came back, late, from the hyacinth
    garden,
Your arms full, and your hair wet, I could not
Speak, and my eyes failed, I was neither
Living nor dead, and I knew nothing,
Looking into the heart of light, the silence.
Oed' und leer das Meer.[9]

Madame Sosostris, famous clairvoyante,
Had a bad cold, nevertheless
Is known to be the wisest woman in Europe,
With a wicked pack of cards.[10] Here, said she,
Is your card, the drowned Phoenician Sailor,
(Those are pearls that were his eyes.[11] Look!)
Here is Belladonna, the Lady of the Rocks,
The lady of situations.
Here is the man with three staves, and here the
    Wheel,
And here is the one-eyed merchant, and this card,
Which is blank, is something he carries on his back,
Which I am forbidden to see. I do not find
The Hanged Man. Fear death by water.
I see crowds of people, walking round in a ring.
Thank you. If you see dear Mrs. Equitone,
Tell her I bring the horoscope myself:
One must be so careful these days.

Unreal City,[12]
Under the brown fog of a winter dawn,

A crowd flowed over London Bridge, so many,
I had not thought death had undone so many.[13]
Sighs, short and infrequent, were exhaled,[14]
And each man fixed his eyes before his feet.
Flowed up the hill and down King William Street,
To where Saint Mary Woolnoth kept the hours
With a dead sound on the final stroke of nine.[15]
There I saw one I knew, and stopped him, crying:
    'Stetson!
'You who were with me in the ships at Mylae![16]   70
'That corpse you planted last year in your garden,
'Has it begun to sprout? Will it bloom this year?
'Or has the sudden frost disturbed its bed?
'O keep the Dog far hence, that's friend to men,[17]
'Or with his nails he'll dig it up again!
'You! hypocrite lecteur!—mon semblable,—mon
    frère!'[18]

II. A Game of Chess[1]

The Chair she sat in, like a burnished throne,[2]
Glowed on the marble, where the glass
Held up by standards wrought with fruited vines
From which a golden Cupidon peeped out
(Another hid his eyes behind his wing)
Doubled the flames of sevenbranched candelabra
Reflecting light upon the table as
The glitter of her jewels rose to meet it,
From satin cases poured in rich profusion;
In vials of ivory and coloured glass
Unstoppered, lurked her strange synthetic
        perfumes,
Unguent, powdered, or liquid—troubled, confused
And drowned the sense in odours; stirred by the air
That freshened from the window, these ascended
In fattening the prolonged candle-flames,
Flung their smoke into the laquearia,[3]
Stirring the pattern on the coffered ceiling.
Huge sea-wood fed with copper
Burned green and orange, framed by the coloured
        stone,
In which sad light a carvèd dolphin swam.
Above the antique mantel was displayed
As though a window gave upon the sylvan scene[4]
The change of Philomel,[5] by the barbarous king
So rudely forced; yet there the nightingale[6]
Filled all the desert with inviolable voice
And still she cried, and still the world pursues,
'Jug Jug' to dirty ears.
And other withered stumps of time
Were told upon the walls; staring forms
Leaned out, leaning, hushing the room enclosed.
Footsteps shuffled on the stair.

Under the firelight, under the brush, her hair
Spread out in fiery points
Glowed into words, then would be savagely still.   110

'My nerves are bad to-night. Yes, bad. Stay with me.
'Speak to me. Why do you never speak. Speak.
     'What are you thinking of? What thinking?
     What?
'I never know what you are thinking. Think.'

I think we are in rats' alley[7]
Where the dead men lost their bones.

'What is that noise?'
                    The wind under the door.[8]
'What is that noise now? What is the wind doing?'
                    Nothing again nothing.   120
                              'Do
'You know nothing? Do you see nothing? Do you
     remember
'Nothing?'

     I remember
Those are pearls that were his eyes.[9]
'Are you alive, or not? Is there nothing in your
     head?'

                                        But

O O O O that Shakespeherian Rag[10] —
It's so elegant
So intelligent   130
'What shall I do now? What shall I do?'
'I shall rush out as I am, and walk the street
'With my hair down, so. What shall we do
     to-morrow?
'What shall we ever do?'
                    The hot water at ten.

And if it rains, a closed car at four.
And we shall play a game of chess,
Pressing lidless eyes and waiting for a knock upon
    the door.[11]

When Lil's husband got demobbed,[12] I said—
I didn't mince my words, I said to her myself,
HURRY UP PLEASE ITS TIME[13]
Now Albert's coming back, make yourself a bit
    smart.
He'll want to know what you done with that
    money he gave you
To get yourself some teeth. He did, I was there.
You have them all out, Lil, and get a nice set,
He said, I swear, I can't bear to look at you.
And no more can't I, I said, and think of poor
    Albert,
He's been in the army four years, he wants a good
    time,
And if you don't give it him, there's others will, I
    said.
Oh is there, she said. Something o' that, I said.
Then I'll know who to thank, she said, and give me
    a straight look.
HURRY UP PLEASE ITS TIME
If you don't like it you can get on with it, I said.
Others can pick and choose if you can't.
But if Albert makes off, it won't be for lack of
    telling.
You ought to be ashamed, I said, to look so
    antique.
(And her only thirty-one.)
I can't help it, she said, pulling a long face,
It's them pills I took, to bring it off, she said.
(She's had five already, and nearly died of young
    George.)
The chemist said it would be all right, but I've
    never been the same.

140

150

160

You *are* a proper fool, I said.

Well, if Albert won't leave you alone, there it is, I
said,

What you get married for if you don't want
children?

HURRY UP PLEASE ITS TIME

Well, that Sunday Albert was home, they had a hot
gammon,[14]

And they asked me in to dinner, to get the beauty
of it hot—

HURRY UP PLEASE ITS TIME

HURRY UP PLEASE ITS TIME

Goonight Bill. Goonight Lou. Goonight May.
Goonight.   170

Ta ta. Goonight. Goonight.

Good night, ladies, good night, sweet ladies, good
night, good night.[15]

III. *The Fire Sermon*[1]

The river's tent is broken: the last fingers of leaf
Clutch and sink into the wet bank. The wind
Crosses the brown land, unheard. The nymphs are
    departed.
Sweet Thames, run softly, till I end my song.[2]
The river bears no empty bottles, sandwich papers,
Silk handkerchiefs, cardboard boxes, cigarette ends
Or other testimony of summer nights. The nymphs
    are departed.
And their friends, the loitering heirs of city directors;
Departed, have left no addresses.
By the waters of Leman I sat down and wept . . .[3]
Sweet Thames, run softly till I end my song,
Sweet Thames, run softly, for I speak not loud or long.
But at my back in a cold blast I hear
The rattle of the bones, and chuckle spread from
    ear to ear.

A rat crept softly through the vegetation
Dragging its slimy belly on the bank
While I was fishing in the dull canal
On a winter evening round behind the gashouse
Musing upon the king my brother's wreck
And on the king my father's death before him.[4]
White bodies naked on the low damp ground
And bones cast in a little low dry garret,
Rattled by the rat's foot only, year to year.
But at my back from time to time I hear[5]
The sound of horns and motors,[6] which shall bring
Sweeney to Mrs. Porter in the spring.
O the moon shone bright on Mrs. Porter[7]
And on her daughter
They wash their feet in soda water
Et O ces voix d'enfants, chantant dans la coupole![8]

Twit twit twit
Jug jug jug jug jug jug
So rudely forc'd.
Tereu[9]

Unreal City
Under the brown fog of a winter noon
Mr. Eugenides, the Smyrna merchant
Unshaven, with a pocket full of currants[10]   210
C.i.f. London: documents at sight,
Asked me in demotic[11] French
To luncheon at the Cannon Street Hotel[12]
Followed by a weekend at the Metropole.[13]

At the violet hour, when the eyes and back
Turn upward from the desk, when the human
    engine waits
Like a taxi throbbing waiting,
I Tiresias, though blind, throbbing between two
    lives,[14]
Old man with wrinkled female breasts, can see
At the violet hour, the evening hour that strives   220
Homeward, and brings the sailor home from sea,[15]
The typist home at teatime, clears her breakfast,
    lights
Her stove, and lays out food in tins.
Out of the window perilously spread
Her drying combinations touched by the sun's last
    rays,
On the divan are piled (at night her bed)
Stockings, slippers, camisoles, and stays.
I Tiresias, old man with wrinkled dugs
Perceived the scene, and foretold the rest—
I too awaited the expected guest.   230
He, the young man carbuncular,[16] arrives,
A small house agent's clerk, with one bold stare,
One of the low on whom assurance sits

As a silk hat on a Bradford millionaire.[17]
The time is now propitious, as he guesses,
The meal is ended, she is bored and tired,
Endeavours to engage her in caresses
Which still are unreproved, if undesired.
Flushed and decided, he assaults at once;
Exploring hands encounter no defence;
His vanity requires no response,
And makes a welcome of indifference.
(And I Tiresias have foresuffered all
Enacted on this same divan or bed;
I who have sat by Thebes below the wall
And walked among the lowest of the dead.)
Bestows one final patronising kiss,
And gropes his way, finding the stairs unlit . . .

She turns and looks a moment in the glass,
Hardly aware of her departed lover;
Her brain allows one half-formed thought to
          pass:
'Well now that's done: and I'm glad it's over.'
When lovely woman stoops to folly[18] and
Paces about her room again, alone,
She smoothes her hair with automatic hand,
And puts a record on the gramophone.

'This music crept by me upon the waters'[19]
And along the Strand, up Queen Victoria Street.[20]
O City city, I can sometimes hear
Beside a public bar in Lower Thames Street,[21]
The pleasant whining of a mandoline
And a clatter and a chatter from within
Where fishmen lounge at noon: where the walls
Of Magnus Martyr[22] hold
Inexplicable splendour of Ionian white and gold.

The river sweats[23]
Oil and tar

The barges drift
With the turning tide
Red sails 270
Wide
To leeward, swing on the heavy spar.
The barges wash
Drifting logs
Down Greenwich reach
Past the Isle of Dogs.
           Weialala leia
           Wallala leialala

Elizabeth and Leicester[24]
Beating oars 280
The stern was formed
A gilded shell
Red and gold
The brisk swell
Rippled both shores
Southwest wind
Carried down stream
The peal of bells
White towers
           Weialala leia 290
           Wallala leialala

'Trams and dusty trees.
Highbury bore me. Richmond and Kew[25]
Undid me. By Richmond I raised my knees
Supine on the floor of a narrow canoe.'

'My feet are at Moorgate,[26] and my heart
Under my feet. After the event
He wept. He promised "a new start."
I made no comment. What should I resent?'

'On Margate Sands.[27] 300
I can connect

Nothing with nothing.
The broken fingernails of dirty hands.
My people humble people who expect
Nothing.'
           la la

To Carthage[28] then I came

Burning burning burning burning[29]
O Lord Thou pluckest me out[30]
O Lord Thou pluckest

burning

IV. Death by Water[1]

Phlebas the Phoenician, a fortnight dead,
Forgot the cry of gulls, and the deep sea swell
And the profit and loss.
                A current under sea
Picked his bones in whispers. As he rose and fell
He passed the stages of his age and youth
Entering the whirlpool.
                Gentile or Jew
O you who turn the wheel and look to windward,   320
Consider Phlebas, who was once handsome and
    tall as you.

V. What the Thunder Said[1]

After the torchlight red on sweaty faces
After the frosty silence in the gardens
After the agony in stony places[2]
The shouting and the crying
Prison and palace and reverberation
Of thunder of spring over distant mountains
He who was living is now dead
We who were living are now dying
With a little patience

Here is no water but only rock[3]
Rock and no water and the sandy road
The road winding above among the mountains
Which are mountains of rock without water
If there were water we should stop and drink
Amongst the rock one cannot stop or think
Sweat is dry and feet are in the sand
If there were only water amongst the rock
Dead mountain mouth of carious teeth that
          cannot spit
Here one can neither stand nor lie nor sit
There is not even silence in the mountains
But dry sterile thunder without rain
There is not even solitude in the mountains
But red sullen faces sneer and snarl
From doors of mudcracked houses
                              If there were water

And no rock
If there were rock
And also water
And water
A spring

A pool among the rock
If there were the sound of water only
Not the cicada
And dry grass singing
But sound of water over a rock
Where the hermit-thrush[4] sings in the pine trees
Drip drop drip drop drop drop drop
But there is no water

Who is the third who walks always beside you?[5]   360
When I count, there are only you and I together
But when I look ahead up the white road
There is always another one walking beside you
Gliding wrapt in a brown mantle, hooded
I do not know whether a man or a woman
—But who is that on the other side of you?

What is that sound high in the air[6]
Murmur of maternal lamentation
Who are those hooded hordes swarming
Over endless plains, stumbling in cracked earth   370
Ringed by the flat horizon only
What is the city over the mountains
Cracks and reforms and bursts in the violet air
Falling towers
Jerusalem Athens Alexandria
Vienna London
Unreal

A woman drew her long black hair out tight
And fiddled whisper music on those strings
And bats with baby faces in the violet light   380
Whistled, and beat their wings
And crawled head downward down a blackened
      wall
And upside down in air were towers
Tolling reminiscent bells, that kept the hours

And voices singing out of empty cisterns and
      exhausted wells.

In this decayed hole among the mountains
In the faint moonlight, the grass is singing
Over the tumbled graves, about the chapel
There is the empty chapel, only the wind's home.
It has no windows, and the door swings,
Dry bones can harm no one.
Only a cock stood on the rooftree
Co co rico co co rico[7]
In a flash of lightning. Then a damp gust
Bringing rain

Ganga[8] was sunken, and the limp leaves
Waited for rain, while the black clouds
Gathered far distant, over Himavant.[9]
The jungle crouched, humped in silence.
Then spoke the thunder
Da
Datta:[10] what have we given?
My friend, blood shaking my heart
The awful daring of a moment's surrender
Which an age of prudence can never retract
By this, and this only, we have existed
Which is not to be found in our obituaries
Or in memories draped by the beneficent spider[11]
Or under seals broken by the lean solicitor
In our empty rooms
Da
Dayadhvam: I have heard the key[12]
Turn in the door once and turn once only
We think of the key, each in his prison
Thinking of the key, each confirms a prison
Only at nightfall, aethereal rumours
Revive for a moment a broken Coriolanus[13]
Da
Damyata: The boat responded

Gaily, to the hand expert with sail and oar   420
The sea was calm, your heart would have
    responded
Gaily, when invited, beating obedient
To controlling hands

                          I sat upon the shore
Fishing, with the arid plain behind me[14]
Shall I at least set my lands in order?
London Bridge is falling down falling down falling
    down
Poi s'ascose nel foco che gli affina[15]
Quando fiam uti chelidon[16]—O swallow swallow
Le Prince d'Aquitaine à la tour abolie[17]   430
These fragments I have shored against my ruins
Why then Ile fit you. Hieronymo's mad againe.[18]
Datta. Dayadhvam. Damyata.
        Shantih   shantih   shantih[19]

Notes on The Waste Land

Not only the title, but the plan and a good deal of the incidental symbolism of the poem were suggested by Miss Jessie L. Weston's book on the Grail legend: *From Ritual to Romance* (Cambridge). Indeed, so deeply am I indebted, Miss Weston's book will elucidate the difficulties of the poem much better than my notes can do; and I recommend it (apart from the great interest of the book itself) to any who think such elucidation of the poem worth the trouble. To another work of anthropology I am indebted in general, one which has influenced our generation profoundly; I mean *The Golden Bough*; I have used especially the two volumes *Adonis, Attis, Osiris*. Anyone who is acquainted with these works will immediately recognise in the poem certain references to vegetation ceremonies.

I. The Burial of the Dead

Line 20. Cf. Ezekiel II, i.

23. Cf. Ecclesiastes XII, v.

31. V. Tristan und Isolde, I, verses 5–8.

42. Id. III, verse 24.

46. I am not familiar with the exact constitution of the Tarot pack of cards, from which I have obviously departed to suit my own convenience. The Hanged Man, a member of the traditional pack, fits my purpose in two ways: because he is associated in my mind with the Hanged God of Frazer, and because I associate him with the hooded figure in the passage of the disciples to Emmaus in Part V. The Phoenician Sailor and the Merchant appear later; also the 'crowds of people,' and Death by Water is executed in Part IV. The Man with Three Staves (an authentic member of the Tarot pack) I associate, quite arbitrarily, with the Fisher King himself.

60. Cf. Baudelaire:

'Fourmillante cité, cité pleine de rêves,

'Où le spectre en plein jour raccroche le passant.'

63. Cf. Inferno III, 55–57:

> 'si lunga tratta
> di gente, ch'io non avrei mai creduto
> che morte tanta n'avesse disfatta.'

64. Cf. Inferno IV, 25–27:

> 'Quivi, secondo che per ascoltare,
> 'non avea pianto, ma' che di sospiri,
> 'che l'aura eterna facevan tremare.'

68. A phenomenon which I have often noticed.

74. Cf. the Dirge in Webster's *White Devil*.

76. V. Baudelaire, Preface to *Fleurs du Mal*.

II. A Game of Chess

77. Cf. *Antony and Cleopatra*, II, ii, l. 190.

92. Laquearia. V. *Aeneid*, I, 726:

> dependent lychni laquearibus aureis incensi, et noctem flammis
> funalia vincunt.

98. Sylvan scene. V. Milton, *Paradise Lost*, IV, 140.

99. V. Ovid, *Metamorphoses*, VI, Philomela.

100. Cf. Part III, l. 204.

115. Cf. Part III, l. 195.

118. Cf. Webster: 'Is the wind in that door still?'

126. Cf. Part I, l. 37, 48.

138. Cf. the game of chess in Middleton's *Women beware Women*.

III. The Fire Sermon

176. V. Spenser, *Prothalamion*.

192. Cf. *The Tempest*, I, ii.

196. Cf. Marvell, *To His Coy Mistress*.

197. Cf. Day, *Parliament of Bees*:

> 'When of the sudden, listening, you shall hear,
> 'A noise of horns and hunting, which shall bring
> 'Actaeon to Diana in the spring,
> 'Where all shall see her naked skin . . .'

199. I do not know the origin of the ballad from which these lines are taken: it was reported to me from Sydney, Australia.

202. V. Verlaine, *Parsifal*.

210. The currants were quoted at a price 'carriage and insurance free to London'; and the Bill of Lading etc. were to be handed to the buyer upon payment of the sight draft.

218. Tiresias, although a mere spectator and not indeed a 'character,' is yet the most important personage in the poem, uniting all the rest. Just as the one-eyed merchant, seller of currants, melts into the Phoenician Sailor, and the latter is not wholly distinct from Ferdinand Prince of Naples, so all the women are one woman, and the two sexes meet in Tiresias. What Tiresias *sees*, in fact, is the substance of the poem. The whole passage from Ovid is of great anthropological interest:

> '. . . Cum Iunone iocos et maior vestra profecto est
> Quam, quae contingit maribus,' dixisse, 'voluptas.'
> Illa negat; placuit quae sit sententia docti
> Quaerere Tiresiae: venus huic erat utraque nota.
> Nam duo magnorum viridi coeuntia silva
> Corpora serpentum baculi violaverat ictu
> Deque viro factus, mirabile, femina septem
> Egerat autumnos; octavo rursus eosdem
> Vidit et 'est vestrae si tanta potentia plagae,'
> Dixit 'ut auctoris sortem in contraria mutet,
> Nunc quoque vos feriam!' percussis anguibus isdem
> Forma prior rediit genetivaque venit imago.
> Arbiter hic igitur sumptus de lite iocosa
> Dicta Iovis firmat; gravius Saturnia iusto
> Nec pro materia fertur doluisse suique
> Iudicis aeterna damnavit lumina nocte,
> At pater omnipotens (neque enim licet inrita
>   cuiquam
> Facta dei fecisse deo) pro lumine adempto
> Scire futura dedit poenamque levavit honore.

221. This may not appear as exact as Sappho's lines, but I had in mind the 'longshore' or 'dory' fisherman, who returns at nightfall.

253. V. Goldsmith, the song in *The Vicar of Wakefield*.

257. V. *The Tempest*, as above.

264. The interior of St. Magnus Martyr is to my mind one of the finest among Wren's interiors. See *The Proposed Demolition of Nineteen City Churches*: (P. S. King & Son, Ltd.).

266. The Song of the (three) Thames-daughters begins here. From line 292 to 306 inclusive they speak in turn. V. *Götterdämmerung*, III, i: the Rhine-daughters.

279. V. Froude, *Elizabeth*, Vol. I, ch. iv, letter of De Quadra to Philip of Spain:

'In the afternoon we were in a barge, watching the games on the river. (The queen) was alone with Lord Robert and myself on the poop, when they began to talk nonsense, and went so far that Lord Robert at last said, as I was on the spot there was no reason why they should not be married if the queen pleased.'

293. Cf. *Purgatorio*, V, 133:

'Ricorditi di me, che son la Pia;

'Siena mi fe', disfecemi Maremma.'

307. V. St. Augustine's *Confessions*: 'to Carthage then I came, where a cauldron of unholy loves sang all about mine ears.'

308. The complete text of the Buddha's Fire Sermon (which corresponds in importance to the Sermon on the Mount) from which these words are taken, will be found translated in the late Henry Clarke Warren's *Buddhism in Translation* (Harvard Oriental Series). Mr. Warren was one of the great pioneers of Buddhist studies in the Occident.

309. From St. Augustine's *Confessions* again. The collocation of these two representatives of eastern and western asceticism, as the culmination of this part of the poem, is not an accident.

V. What the Thunder Said

In the first part of Part V three themes are employed: the journey to Emmaus, the approach to the Chapel Perilous (see Miss Weston's book) and the present decay of eastern Europe.

357. This is *Turdus aonalaschkae pallasii*, the hermit-thrush which I have heard in Quebec Province. Chapman says (*Handbook of Birds of*

Eastern North America) 'it is most at home in secluded woodland and thickety retreats. . . . Its notes are not remarkable for variety or volume, but in purity and sweetness of tone and exquisite modulation they are unequalled.' Its 'water-dripping song' is justly celebrated.

360. The following lines were stimulated by the account of one of the Antarctic expeditions (I forget which, but I think one of Shackleton's): it was related that the party of explorers, at the extremity of their strength, had the constant delusion that there was *one more member* than could actually be counted.

367–77. Cf. Hermann Hesse, *Blick ins Chaos*: 'Schon ist halb Europa, schon ist zumindest der halbe Osten Europas auf dem Wege zum Chaos, fährt betrunken im heiligem Wahn am Abgrund entlang und singt dazu, singt betrunken und hymnisch wie Dmitri Karamasoff sang. Ueber diese Lieder lacht der Bürger beleidigt, der Heilige und Seher hört sie mit Tränen.'

402. 'Datta, dayadhvam, damyata' (Give, sympathise, control). The fable of the meaning of the Thunder is found in the *Brihadaranyaka— Upanishad*, 5, 1. A translation is found in Deussen's *Sechzig Upanishads des Veda*, p. 489.

408. Cf. Webster, *The White Devil*, V, vi:

'. . . they'll remarry

Ere the worm pierce your winding-sheet, ere the spider
Make a thin curtain for your epitaphs.'

412. Cf. *Inferno*, XXXIII, 46:

'ed io sentii chiavar l'uscio di sotto
all'orribile torre.'

Also F. H. Bradley, *Appearance and Reality*, p. 346.

'My external sensations are no less private to myself than are my thoughts or my feelings. In either case my experience falls within my own circle, a circle closed on the outside; and, with all its elements alike, every sphere is opaque to the others which surround it. . . . In brief, regarded as an existence which appears in a soul, the whole world for each is peculiar and private to that soul.'

425. V. Weston: *From Ritual to Romance*; chapter on the Fisher King.

428. V. *Purgatorio*, XXVI, 148.

' "Ara vos prec per aquella valor
"que vos guida al som de l'escalina,

"sovegna vos a temps de ma dolor."
Poi s'ascose nel foco che gli affina.'

429. V. *Pervigilium Veneris*. Cf. Philomela in Parts II and III.

430. V. Gerard de Nerval, Sonnet *El Desdichado*.

432. V. Kyd's *Spanish Tragedy*.

434. Shantih. Repeated as here, a formal ending to an Upanishad. 'The Peace which passeth understanding' is our equivalent to this word.

Endnotes

Prufrock and Other Observations

DEDICATION

1. (p. 5) *Jean Verdenal, 1889–1915 mort aux Dardanelles*: Verdenal was a friend of Eliot's from Paris, and the first person he knew who was killed in World War I ('died at Dardanelles').

2. (p. 5) *Or puoi quantitante . . . come cosa salda*: The quotation is from Dante's *Purgatorio*, 21.132–135: 'Now you can understand the quantity of love that warms me toward you, so that I forget our vanity, and treat the shades as the solid thing.'

'THE LOVE SONG OF J. ALFRED PRUFROCK'

1. (p. 9) S'io credessi . . . ti rispondo: The quotation is from Dante's *Inferno*, 27.61–66. Dante asks one of the damned souls for its name, and the reply is: 'If I thought my answer were for one who might return to the world, this flame would remain without further movement. But as none ever return alive from this depth, if what I hear is true, I may answer you without fear of infamy.' The soul is, of course, mistaken that none return from Hell: Dante himself will do so.

2. (p. 9) *In the room the women come and go / Talking of Michelangelo*: The reference is to the great Italian Renaissance sculptor and painter (1475–1564); implicitly, the speaker suggests that the women have no business talking of him or are unlikely to say anything profound.

3. (p. 10) *And indeed there will be time*: Eliot's repetition of 'time' in this passage echoes both Andrew Marvell's poem 'To His Coy Mistress' ('Had we but world enough, and time . . .') and the Bible (Ecclesiastes 3:1–8: 'To every thing there is a season, and a time to every purpose under the heaven: A time to be born, and a time to die . . .' [King James Version; henceforth, KJV]).

4. (p. 10) *works and days*: Greek writer Hesiod (eighth century B.C.) wrote *Works and Days*, a poem that offers maxims and practical instruction to farmers.

5. (p. 10) *a dying fall*: Eliot here echoes a phrase from Shakespeare's *Twelfth Night* (act 1, scene 1): 'If music be the food of love, play on; / Give me excess of it, that, surfeiting, / The appetite may sicken, and so die. / That strain again! it had a dying fall.'

6. (p. 12) *my head . . . brought in upon a platter*: Matthew 14:3–11 describes how Salomé danced for Herod and was rewarded with the head of the prophet John the Baptist, brought in upon a platter.

7. (p. 12) *into a ball*: Compare Marvell's 'To His Coy Mistress': 'Let us roll all our strength and all / Our sweetness up into one ball' to send against the 'iron gates of life.'

8. (p. 12) *I am Lazarus, come from the dead*: In the Bible, John 11:1–44 tells of how Lazarus was raised from the dead.

9. (p. 12) *magic lantern*: This type of slide projector dates back to the seventeenth century; images were painted onto glass and projected on a wall by the light of a candle.

10. (p. 13) *Prince Hamlet*: For Eliot's idiosyncratic appraisal of Shakespeare's tragic hero, in which he judges the entire play to be an artistic failure, see his 1919 essay 'Hamlet and His Problems' (see 'For Further Reading').

11. (p. 13) *the Fool*: A stock figure in Elizabethan drama, the Fool often spoke nonsense but sometimes conveyed subtle, indirect insights.

12. (p. 13) *I have heard the mermaids singing*: The line echoes seventeenth-century poet John Donne's 'Song': 'Teach me to heare Mermaides singing.'

'PORTRAIT OF A LADY'

1. (p. 14) Thou hast committed— . . . THE JEW OF MALTA: In this dialogue from the play (act 4, scene 1) by Christopher Marlowe (1564–1593), a Friar accuses Barabas, the title character, who interrupts and completes the statement with his own words.

2. (p. 14) *Juliet's tomb*: In Shakespeare's *Romeo and Juliet*, Juliet's tomb is the site of Romeo's tragically mistaken surmise that Juliet is dead, precipitating his own suicide.

3. (p. 14) *Preludes*: Polish composer Frédéric Chopin (1810–1849) wrote piano pieces called preludes.

4. (p. 14) *velleities*: This seventeenth-century word signifies desires, without any action to bring them to reality.

5. (p. 15) cauchemar: The word is French for 'nightmare.'

6. (p. 15) *ariettes*: Lively light tunes.

7. (p. 15) *bocks*: Bock is a type of dark, strong German beer.

8. (p. 17) *friends*: This dialogue is evocative of a scene in Henry James's novel *The Ambassadors* (1903): Madame de Vionnet's parting words to Strether are 'we might, you and I, have been friends.' The poem's title evokes James's *The Portrait of a Lady* (1881).

9. (p. 18) a 'dying fall': As in 'The Love Song of J. Alfred Prufrock' (see note 5 to that poem), this phrase evokes a line from Shakespeare's *Twelfth Night* (act 1, scene 1).

'RHAPSODY ON A WINDY NIGHT'

1. (p. 21) *a lunar synthesis*: This and many other images in the poem—the geranium, the disembodied eyes—evoke the style of French Symbolist poet Jules Laforgue (1860–1887).
2. (p. 21) *Dissolve the floors of memory*: This concept, explained by Henri Bergson (1859–1941), a philosopher at the Sorbonne with whom Eliot studied, involves the free flow of images into the memory, where they combine. All references to memory in this poem are influenced by Bergsonian philosophy.
3. (p. 21) *'Regard that woman...'*: For this figure, and much of the poem's late-night seedy atmosphere, Eliot is indebted to Charles-Louis Philippe's 1901 novel *Bubu de Montparnasse*, about a young prostitute.

'THE BOSTON EVENING TRANSCRIPT'

1. (p. 25) *La Rochefoucauld*: French author François La Rochefoucauld (1613–1680) is best known for his *maximes*, epigrams expressing a harsh or paradoxical truth in the briefest manner possible.

'COUSIN NANCY'

1. (p. 27) *Matthew and Waldo*: Eliot perhaps intends Matthew Arnold (1822–1888) and Ralph Waldo Emerson (1803–1882) as competing British and American emblems of Victorian propriety.

'MR. APOLLINAX'

1. (p. 28) *Ω τῆς καινότητος. Ἡράκλεις, τῆς παραδοξολογίας. εὐμήχανο ἄνθρωπος....* LUCIAN: From the second-century Greek historian's 'Zeuxis or Antiochus': 'What an ingenious fellow!'
2. (p. 28) *Mr. Apollinax*: The poem's title character is a caricature of Bertrand Russell (1872–1970), the Harvard philosopher and mathematician with whom Eliot studied.
3. (p. 18) *Priapus*: This Roman fertility god was mainly known for his huge phallus. All the other characters named in this poem are Eliot's inventions.

'CONVERSATION GALANTE'

1. (p. 31) *Prester John's*: Prester (Priest) John was a legendary Christian king of the east.

'LA FIGLIA CHE PIANGE'

1. (p. 32) La Figlia che Piange: The title is Italian for 'The Weeping Girl.'

2. (p. 32) *O quam te memorem virgo . . .*: The epigraph is a quotation from Virgil's *Aeneid* 1.327: 'O maiden, by what name shall I know you?' Eliot's poem was inspired by a scene on a stele (a sculptured or inscribed stone slab used as a monument) that Eliot had been told to see on a trip to Italy but was unable to find.

Poems 1920

'GERONTION'

1. (p. 37) *Gerontion*: The word is Greek for 'little old man.'
2. (p. 37) *Thou hast . . . of both*: The lines are slightly misquoted from Shakespeare's *Measure for Measure* (act 3, scene 1).
3. (p. 37) *estaminet*: Café.
4. (p. 37) *'We would see a sign!'*: In the Bible (Matthew 12:38–39), the Pharisees called upon Christ to demonstrate his divinity by performing a miracle. Eliot's source is a 1618 Nativity Sermon by Bishop Lancelot Andrewes.
5. (p. 37) *judas*: This tree—named after Judas Iscariot, the apostle who betrayed Jesus—is reputed to be the type of tree from which he hanged himself.
6. (p. 38) *Limoges*: This French city is renowned for its China.
7. (p. 38) *Fräulein von Kulp*: This and the other proper names in this passage (excepting Titian, an Italian Renaissance painter, c.1485–1576) are characters Eliot invented; their names are meant to suggest dubious foreigners who are perhaps participating in some sort of séance.
8. (p. 38) *contrived corridors*: Perhaps Eliot means to evoke the Polish Corridor, a piece of land taken from Germany and given to Poland under the Treaty of Versailles (1919) that followed the end of World War I. Eliot would probably concur with the judgment of many historians that the treaty carved up Europe in a way which was politically and culturally unstable, and that it effected only a temporary peace which led to the resumption of European conflict in World War II.
9. (p. 38) *weak hands*: The phrase echoes Percy Bysshe Shelley's *Adonais* (stanza 27).
10. (p. 38) *the wrath-bearing tree*: Perhaps Eliot is referring to the tree of knowledge of good and evil in the Garden of Eden.
11. (p. 39) *De Bailhache, Fresca, Mrs. Cammel*: Again, these are fictitious figures.
12. (p. 39) *Bear*: Eliot is referring to the constellation Ursa Major (also known as the Big Dipper).

13. (p. 39) *the windy straits / Of Belle Isle*: The Strait of Belle Isle is a passage in eastern Canada, between Newfoundland and Labrador, that connects the Atlantic Ocean with the Gulf of St. Lawrence; the cold Labrador Current flows through the strait.

14. (p. 39) *the Horn*: Cape Horn is a rocky headland off the southern tip of South America.

15. (p. 39) *the Trades*: That is, the trade winds, steady westward winds that blow toward the equator.

'BURBANK WITH A BAEDEKER: BLEISTEIN WITH A CIGAR'

1. (p. 40) *Burbank with a Baedeker: Bleistein with a Cigar*: A Baedeker is a tourist guidebook. Burbank and Bleistein are made-up American characters.

2. (p. 40) Tra-la-la-la-la-la-laire . . . and so departed: The epigraph contains fragments from six texts connected with Venice, by Théophile Gautier, Mantegna, Henry James (*The Aspern Papers*), Shakespeare (*Othello*), Robert Browning ('A Toccata of Galuppi's'), and John Marston.

3. (p. 40) *Princess Volupine*: Princess Volupine and, near the end of the poem, Sir Ferdinand Klein are Eliot's inventions.

4. (p. 40) *They were together, and he fell*: Echoes a line from 'The Sisters,' by Alfred Lord Tennyson (1809–1892).

5. (p. 40) *the God Hercules*: This mythical hero (Hercules to the Romans, Heracles to the Greeks) possessed fabulous strength; he performed twelve monumental tasks ('the labors of Hercules') that earned him immortality and the status of a god.

6. (p. 40) *Istria*: City near Venice, in present-day Croatia.

7. (p. 40) *Canaletto*: Giovanni Antonio Canale (1697–1768), known by the nickname Canaletto, painted many views of the Venetian canals.

8. (p. 40) *Rialto*: This ancient district of Venice is the city's commercial center.

9. (p. 41) *lion's wings*: A winged lion is the emblem of Saint Mark, patron saint of Venice.

'SWEENEY ERECT'

1. (p. 42) And the trees . . . wenches!: The quotation is from *The Maides Tragedy* (c.1611; act 2, scene 2), by Francis Beaumont and John Fletcher.

2. (p. 42) *Cyclades*: This group of Greek islands is in the Aegean Sea.

3. (p. 42) *Aeolus*: Greek god of the winds.

4. (p. 42) *Ariadne*: In Greek myth, daughter of King Minos of Crete; in love with the hero Theseus, she helped him find his way in and out of the labyrinth.

5. (p. 42) *Nausicaa*: In Greek myth, this king's daughter discovered Odysseus when he was shipwrecked and cast up upon the shore.

6. (p. 42) *Polypheme*: In Greek myth, he was the leader of the Cyclopes, a race of one-eyed giants.

7. (p. 43) *Emerson*: Eliot paraphrases Ralph Waldo Emerson's essay 'Self-Reliance' (1841): 'an institution is the lengthened shadow of one man.'

'A COOKING EGG'

1. (p. 44) *A Cooking Egg*: An egg too stale to be eaten plain, but usable in a recipe.

2. (p. 44) *En l'an trentiesme . . . j'ay beues . . .* : The lines are by French lyric poet François Villon (1431–after 1463): 'In my thirtieth year, when I drank up all my shame . . .'

3. (p. 44) *Invitation to the Dance*: Sheet music for a nineteenth-century song.

4. (p. 44) *Sir Philip Sidney*: English poet and statesman (1554–1586) of the Elizabethan era.

5. (p. 44) *Coriolanus*: Hero of Shakespeare's play of that name—a Roman general.

6. (p. 44) *Sir Alfred Mond*: Mond (1868–1930) was a wealthy British industrialist; his Jewish heritage prompts a stereotypical slur here.

7. (p. 44) *Lucretia Borgia*: Borgia (1480–1519), duchess of Ferrara, was intimate with many noble Italian families.

8. (p. 44) *Madame Blavatsky*: Russian-born Helena Petrovna Blavatsky (1831–1891) was a spiritualist who in 1875 organized the Theosophical Society.

9. (p. 44) *Seven Sacred Trances*: Part of the secret doctrines of Theosophy.

10. (p. 44) *Piccarda de Donati*: Figure from canto 3 of Dante's *Paradiso*: a nun who broke her vows.

11. (p. 45) *penny world*: A bakery sweet treat.

12. (p. 45) *Kentish Town and Golder's Green*: Northern suburbs of London.

13. (p. 45) *A.B.C.'s*: The Aerated Bread Company, a chain of English tea shops.

'LE DIRECTEUR'

1. (p. 46) *Le Directeur*: French for 'The Director.' English translation by Annie Sokolov-Uris and Robert G. Uris:

> *Woe unto the woeful Thames*
> *Which runs so close to the Spectator.*

> *The director*
> *Conservative*
> *Of the Spectator*
> *Infects the breeze.*
> *The stockholders*
> *Reactionaries*
> *Of the Spectator*
> *Conservative*
> *Arm in arm*
> *Playing tricks*
> *With slinking steps.*
> *In a gutter*
> *A little girl*
> *In rags*
> *Grimly*
> *Looks at*
> *The director*
> *Of the Spectator*
> *Conservative*
> *And dies of love.*

2. (p. 46) *Spectateur*: *The Spectator*, a highbrow London weekly magazine.

'MÉLANGE ADULTÈRE DE TOUT'

1. (p. 47) *Mélange adultère de tout*: French for 'Adulterous Mixture of Everything.' English translation by Annie Sokolov-Uris and Robert G. Uris:

> *In America, professor;*
> *In England, journalist;*
> *It is with big steps and in a sweat*
> *That you barely follow my tracks.*
> *In Yorkshire, lecturer;*
> *In London, a little bit of a banker,*
> *You will pay me well by the head.*
> *It is in Paris that I get my hairdo*
> *Black helmet of a carefree person.*
> *In Germany, philosopher*
> *Over-excited by Emporheben*
> *With the grand air of Bergsteigleben;*

I always wander from here to there
With some tra là là
From Damascus to Omaha.
I will celebrate my saint's day
In an African oasis
Clothed in a giraffe's skin.

One will show my cenotaph
On the burning coast of Mozambique.

'LUNE DE MIEL'

1. (p. 48) *Lune de miel*: French for 'Honeymoon.' English translation by
   Annie Sokolov-Uris and Robert G. Uris:

   They saw the Low Countries, they returned to Terre Haute;
   But one summer night, here they are in Ravenna,
   At ease between two sheets, in the home of two hundred
   *   bedbugs.*
   The summer sweat, and a strong odor of bitch.
   They stay on their backs their knees spread
   From four flabby legs completely swollen from bites.
   One lifts the sheet to scratch better.
   Less than a league from here is Saint Apollinaire
   In class, a basilica known by lovers
   Of acanthus columns with winds swirling around.

   They are going to take the eight o'clock train
   To prolong their misery from Padua to Milan
   Where one finds The Last Supper, and a cheap restaurant.
   He thinks about tips, and draws up his balance sheet.
   They will have seen Switzerland and crossed France.
   And Saint Apollinaire, stiff and ascetic,
   Old deconsecrated factory, still holding
   In its crumbling stones the precise form of Byzantium.

'THE HIPPOPOTAMUS'

1. (p. 49) *The Hippopotamus*: A parody of 'L'Hippopotame,' by
   Théophile Gautier (1811–1872).
2. (p. 49) Similiter et omnes . . . *S. IGNATII AD TRALLIANOS*: In like man-
   ner let all men respect the deacons as Jesus Christ, even as they should

respect the bishop as being a type of the Father and the presbyters as the council of God and as the college of Apostles. Apart from these there is not even the name of a church. And I am persuaded that ye are so minded as touching these matters. Saint Ignatius to the Trallians.

3. (p. 49) And when this epistle . . . church of the Laodiceans: From the Bible, St. Paul's epistle to the Colossians 4:16.

4. (p. 49) *based upon a rock*: In the Bible (Matthew 16:18), Christ says, 'Thou art Peter, and upon this rock I will build my church' (KJV).

5. (p. 50) *quiring*: Choiring.

'DANS LE RESTAURANT'

1. (p. 51) *Dans le Restaurant*: French for 'In the Restaurant.' English translation by Annie Sokolov-Uris and Robert G. Uris:

> *The dilapidated waiter who has nothing to do*
> *But to scratch his fingers and lean on my shoulder:*
> *'In my country the weather will be rainy,*
> *Some wind, some strong sun and some rain;*
> *It is what one calls the tramp's laundry day.'*
> *(Chatterbox, drooling, with a rounded rump,*
> *I beg you, at least, don't drool in the soup).*
> *'The wet willow, and some buds on the roots.*
> *It is here, in a downpour, where you find shelter.*
> *I was seven, she was younger.*
> *She was all wet, I gave her some primroses.'*
> *The spots on his vest summed to thirty-eight.*
> *'I would tickle her to make her laugh.*
> *I felt a moment of power and delirium.'*
>
> *But then, lubricious old man, at your age . . .*
> *'Sir, the fact is hard.*
> *He came, to hug us, a big dog;*
> *I was afraid, I left him halfway.*
> *It's a shame.'*
> *But then you have your vulture!*
> *Go and wipe the wrinkles off your face;*
> *Here, my fork, scrape away the dirt from your skull.*
> *By what right are you paying for experiences like me?*
> *Hold on, here are ten sous, for the bathroom.*

> Phlebas, the Phoenician, a fortnight dead,
> Forgot the cry of gulls and the wind's howl of
>   Cornwall,
> And the profit and loss, and the cargo ships of pewter:
> An undertow took him far away,
> Passing the stages of his former life.
> Go figure, it was a hard fate;
> Nevertheless, he was once a handsome man, of great
>   stature.

'WHISPERS OF IMMORTALITY'

1. (p. 53) *Webster*: English dramatist John Webster (c.1580–c.1625).
2. (p. 53) *Donne*: English metaphysical poet John Donne (1572–1631).
3. (p. 53) *Grishkin*: Based on the character of the Russian dancer Serafima Astafieva (1876–1934).
4. (p. 54) *Abstract Entities*: Philosophical ideas about existence.

'MR. ELIOT'S SUNDAY MORNING SERVICE'

1. (p. 55) Look, look, master . . . *THE JEW OF MALTA*: From the play (act 4, scene 1) by Christopher Marlowe (1564–1593).
2. (p. 55) *Polyphiloprogenitive*: A word of Eliot's invention, meaning highly fecund or fertile.
3. (p. 55) *sutlers*: Provision merchants to an army.
4. (p. 55) *Superfetation*: Multiple impregnation resulting in the birth of more than one child.
5. (p. 55) τὸ ἕν: The Greek words translate as 'the one.'
6. (p. 55) *mensual*: Monthly.
7. (p. 55) *Origen*: Early Christian theological writer (c. A.D. 185–254).
8. (p. 55) *the Umbrian school*: School of painting from fifteenth-century Italy.
9. (p. 55) *a gesso ground*: Plaster surface for murals.
10. (p. 55) *nimbus*: Halo.
11. (p. 55) *the Paraclete*: The Holy Ghost.
12. (p. 55) *sable presbyters*: Black-robed priests.
13. (p. 55) *piaculative pence*: Collection money, which the pimply ('pustular') youth hope will expiate (piaculate) their sins.
14. (p. 55) *Seraphim*: Angels.
15. (p. 56) *Along the garden-wall . . . / The staminate and pistillate*: These lines describe the process of pollination.
16. (p. 56) *epicene*: Having characteristics of both sexes.
17. (p. 56) *polymath*: Having great and varied learning.

'SWEENEY AMONG THE NIGHTINGALES'

1. (p. 57) *Nightingales*: Slang for prostitutes.
2. (p. 57) ὤμοι, πέπληγμαι καιρίαν πληγὴν ἔσω: 'Alas, I am struck deep with a mortal blow,' the words of Agamemnon as he is slain by his wife, Clytemnestra, in *Agamemnon*, by Aeschylus (525–456 B.C.).
3. (p. 57) *maculate*: Polluted.
4. (p. 57) *River Plate*: In Spanish this is the Río de la Plata, a broad inlet of the Atlantic Ocean that separates Uruguay and Argentina.
5. (p. 57) *Gloomy Orion*: Eliot took the phrase from Christopher Marlowe's *Dido, Queen of Carthage* (1594; act 1, scene 2). The constellation of Orion includes Sirius, the Dog Star.
6. (p. 57) *murderous paws*: This image is also taken from *Dido* (see note just above; act 2, scene 1), in a description of the Myrmidons, a warlike race.
7. (p. 58) *Convent of the Sacred Heart*: Convent of nuns, the Roman Catholic congregation of the Sisters of the Sacred Heart of Jesus and Mary.
8. (p. 58) *Agamemnon*: See epigraph.

The Waste Land

DEDICATION

1. (p. 61) '*Nam Sibyllam* . . . ἀποθανειν θέλω': 'I saw with my own eyes the Sibyl hanging in a cage, and when the boys cried at her, "Sybil, what do you want?" she responded, "I wish I were dead."' From the *Satyricon*, by Petronius (first century A.D.). Sybils were women believed to have prophetic powers; they were gatekeepers to the underworld.
2. (p. 61) il miglior fabbro: 'The better craftsman,' from Dante's *Purgatorio* 34.117. American poet and critic Ezra Pound (1885–1972) was a friend and supporter of Eliot's, and a fellow American expatriate in Europe. Eliot appreciated greatly his editing of the poem's manuscript.

'I. THE BURIAL OF THE DEAD'

1. (p. 65) *The Burial of the Dead*: This is the title of the Church of England's burial service.
2. (p. 65) *April is the cruellest month*: Compare the opening lines of the General Prologue in *The Canterbury Tales*, by Geoffrey Chaucer (c.1343–1400):

When that April, with his showers swoot [sweet],
The drought of March hath pierced to the root,
And bathed every vein in such licour,
Of which virtue engender'd is the flower;
When Zephyrus eke with his swoote breath
Inspired hath in every holt [forest] and heath
The tender croppes [boughs] and the younge sun
Hath in the Ram his halfe course y-run,
And smalle fowles make melody . . .'

3. (p. 65) *Starnbergersee*: Lake resort near Munich.

4. (p. 65) *Hofgarten*: Park in Munich.

5. (p. 65) *Bin gar . . . echt deutsch*: The German line translates as 'I am not Russian at all; I come from Lithuania, a real German.'

6. (p. 65) *Son of man*: See Eliot's note to line 20. The line from Ezekiel reads: 'And he said unto me, Son of man, stand upon thy feet, and I will speak unto thee' (KJV).

7. (p. 65) *the dead tree gives no shelter, the cricket no relief*: See Eliot's note to line 23. The line from Ecclesiastes reads: 'Also when they shall be afraid of that which is high, and fears shall be in the way, and the almond tree shall flourish, and the grasshopper shall be a burden, and desire shall fail: because man goeth to his long home, and the mourners go about the streets' (KJV).

8. (p. 66) *Frisch weht der Wind / . . . Wo weilist du?*: The German lines translate as 'Fresh blows the wind toward home. My Irish child, where are you waiting?' See Eliot's note to line 31.

9. (p. 66) *Oed' und leer das Meer*: The German line translates as 'Empty and waste is the sea.' See Eliot's note to line 42.

10. (p. 66) *a wicked pack of cards*: See Eliot's note to line 46.

11. (p. 66) *Those are pearls that were his eyes*: Line 3 of the second part of Ariel's song in Shakespeare's *Tempest* (act 1, scene 2).

12. (p. 66) *Unreal City*: See Eliot's note to line 60. The lines of French poet Charles Baudelaire translate as: 'Swarming city, city full of dreams, / where the specter in broad daylight accosts the passerby.'

13. (p. 67) *I had not thought death had undone so many*: See Eliot's note to line 63. Dante, just outside the gate of hell, has seen 'the wretched souls of those who lived without disgrace and without praise.'

14. (p. 67) *Sighs, short and infrequent, were exhaled*: See Eliot's note to line 64. The lines from *Inferno* translate as: 'Here, as far as I could tell by listening, there was no lamentation except sighs which caused the eternal air to tremble.'

15. (p. 67) *With a dead sound on the final stroke of nine*: See Eliot's note to line 68.

16. (p. 67) *at Mylae*: Sicilian port, site of the battle of Mylae (260 B.C.), in which Rome gained dominance over Carthage in Sicilian waters.

17. (p. 67) *'keep the Dog far hence, that's friend to men'*: See Eliot's note to line 74.

18. (p. 67) *'hypocrite lecteur!—mon semblable,—mon frère!'*: The French translates as 'Hypocrite reader!—my likeness,—my brother!' See Eliot's note to line 76.

'II. A GAME OF CHESS'

1. (p. 68) *A Game of Chess*: Allusion to *A Game at Chesse* (1624), by English dramatist Thomas Middleton.

2. (p. 68) *The Chair she sat in, like a burnished throne*: See Eliot's note to line 77. In Shakespeare's play, Enobarbus describes Cleopatra:

> The barge she sat in, like a burnish'd throne,
> Burn'd on the water; the poop was beaten gold,
> Purple the sails, and so perfumed, that
> The winds were love-sick with them, the oars were silver,
> Which to the tune of flutes kept stroke, and made
> The water which they beat to follow faster,
> As amorous of their strokes. For her own person,
> It beggar'd all description; she did lie
> In her pavilion,—cloth-of-gold of tissue,—
> O'er-picturing that Venus where we see
> The fancy outwork nature; on each side her
> Stood pretty-dimpled boys, like smiling Cupids,
> With divers-colour'd fans, whose wind did seem
> To glow the delicate cheeks which they did cool,
> And what they undid did.

3. (p. 68) *laquearia*: Paneled ceiling. See Eliot's note to line 92. The lines from Virgil's *Aeneid* translate as: 'Blazing torches hang from the gold-paneled ceiling, and torches conquer the night with flames.'

4. (p. 68) *sylvan scene*: See Eliot's note to line 98. The lines from *Paradise Lost* read:

> . . . and overhead upgrew
> Insuperable height of loftiest shade,
> Cedar, and pine, and fir, and branching palm,
> A sylvan scene, and, as the ranks ascend,
> Shade above shade, a woody theatre
> Of stateliest view. Yet higher than their tops
> The verdurous wall of Paradise upsprung.

5. (p. 68) *Philomel*: Philomela, a character in Ovid's *Metamorphoses*, is raped by her brother-in-law and has her tongue cut out so that she cannot tell her story, but she weaves a tapestry that condemns her assailant. See Eliot's note to line 99.

6. (p. 68) *nightingale*: Philomela metamorphosed into a nightingale. See Eliot's note to line 100.

7. (p. 69) *rats' alley*: Slang for the trenches of World War I. See Eliot's note to line 115.

8. (p. 69) *the wind under the door*: See Eliot's note to line 118. The line is from John Webster's *The Devil's Lawcase* (1623; act 3, scene 2).

9. (p. 69) *Those are pearls that were his eyes*: See Eliot's note to line 126.

10. (p. 69) *Shakespeherian Rag*: A contemporary popular ragtime song.

11. (p. 70) *Pressing . . . door*: See Eliot's note to line 138.

12. (p. 70) *demobbed*: Demobilized (discharged from service) after World War I.

13. (p. 70) *HURRY UP PLEASE ITS TIME*: Last call for drinks at a pub.

14. (p. 71) *gammon*: Smoked ham.

15. (p. 71) *Good night . . . good night*: Ophelia's farewell before drowning, in *Hamlet* (act 4, scene 5).

'III. THE FIRE SERMON'

1. (p. 72) *The Fire Sermon*: The reference is to the Buddha's Fire Sermon, in which he says that the body and its sensations as well as the mind and its ideas are aflame with passion and emotion, and thus should be ignored by those seeking enlightenment.

2. (p. 72) *Sweet Thames, run softly, till I end my song*: See Eliot's note to line 176.

3. (p. 72) *By the waters of Leman I sat down and wept . . .*: This line echoes the lament of the exiled Jews in Psalm 137: 'By the rivers of Babylon, there we sat down, yea, we wept, when we remembered Zion' (KJV). Lac Léman is Lake Geneva in Lausanne, Switzerland, where Eliot wrote much of this poem while recuperating from his nervous breakdown.

4. (p. 72) *And on the king my father's death before him*: See Eliot's note to line 192.

5. (p. 72) *at my back from time to time I hear*: See Eliot's note to line 196. Marvell wrote: 'But at my back I always hear / Time's winged chariot hurrying near.'

6. (p. 72) *the sound of horns and motors*: See Eliot's note to line 197.

7. (p. 72) *Mrs. Porter*: The line is from a bawdy World War I soldiers' song. See Eliot's note to line 199.

8. (p. 72) Et O ces voix d'enfants, chantant dans la coupole!: 'And O those children's voices singing in the dome!' See Eliot's note to line

202. French lyric poet Paul Verlaine (1844–1896) was a leading Symbolist.

9. (p. 73) *Tereu*: King Tereus, who raped Philomela (see line 99).

10. (p. 73) *currants*: See Eliot's note to line 210.

11. (p. 73) *demotic*: Colloquial.

12. (p. 73) *Cannon Street Hotel*: The hotel was at London's Cannon Street Station, the main terminus for business travelers to and from continental Europe.

13. (p. 73) *the Metropole*: This luxury resort hotel was at Brighton, on England's south coast.

14. (p. 73) *Tiresias, though blind, throbbing between two lives*: The Greek mythic character Tiresias experienced life as both a woman and a man, in order to adjudicate the question of which sex was more sexually fulfilled, and ultimately decided that women were. See Eliot's note to line 218, which conveys an important insight about the poem's narrative perspective: All the characters in the poem are, in a sense, united, so that what seems like a dazzling multiplicity of viewpoints may actually be regarded as a single, coherent vision. The lines were translated by John Dryden and Alexander Pope as:

> *'Twas now, while these transactions past on Earth,*
> *And Bacchus thus procur'd a second birth,*
> *When Jove, dispos'd to lay aside the weight*
> *Of publick empire and the cares of state,*
> *As to his queen in nectar bowls he quaff'd,*
> *'In troth,' says he, and as he spoke he laugh'd,*
> *'The sense of pleasure in the male is far*
> *More dull and dead, than what you females share.'*
> *Juno the truth of what was said deny'd;*
> *Tiresias therefore must the cause decide,*
> *For he the pleasure of each sex had try'd.*
> *It happen'd once, within a shady wood,*
> *Two twisted snakes he in conjunction view'd,*
> *When with his staff their slimy folds he broke,*
> *And lost his manhood at the fatal stroke.*
> *But, after seven revolving years, he view'd*
> *The self-same serpents in the self-same wood:*
> *'And if,' says he, 'such virtue in you lye,*
> *That he who dares your slimy folds untie*
> *Must change his kind, a second stroke I'll try.'*
> *Again he struck the snakes, and stood again*

New-sex'd, and strait recover'd into man.

Him therefore both the deities create

The sov'raign umpire, in their grand debate;

And he declar'd for Jove: when Juno fir'd,

More than so trivial an affair requir'd,

Depriv'd him, in her fury, of his sight,

And left him groping round in sudden night.

But Jove (for so it is in Heav'n decreed,

That no one God repeal another's deed)

Irradiates all his soul with inward light,

And with the prophet's art relieves the want of sight.

15. (p. 73) *Homeward, and brings the sailor home from sea*: See Eliot's note to line 221.

16. (p. 73) *carbuncular*: The word 'carbuncle' may describe a precious gem, but here the meaning is more pedestrian—pimply.

17. (p. 74) *a Bradford millionaire*: Bradford is a manufacturing town in northern England that created many wealthy people, whom Eliot regards as nouveaux riche.

18. (p. 74) *When lovely woman stoops to folly*: See Eliot's note to line 253.

19. (p. 74) *'This music crept by me upon the waters'*: See Eliot's note to line 257.

20. (p. 74) *along the Strand, up Queen Victoria Street*: These locations are in the City of London, the financial district, where Eliot was then working.

21. (p. 74) *Lower Thames Street*: Near London Bridge.

22. (p. 74) *Magnus Martyr*: See Eliot's note to line 264.

23. (p. 74) *The river sweats*: See Eliot's note to line 266. *Götterdämmerung* (*The Twilight of the Gods*; first performed in 1876) is the fourth part of Wagner's *Der Ring des Nibelungen* (*The Ring of the Nibelung*). In *Götterdämmerung* a stolen magic golden ring is returned to the Rhine Maidens.

24. (p. 75) *Leicester*: Lord Robert Dudley, earl of Leicester, was rumored to be Queen Elizabeth's lover. See Eliot's note to line 279.

25. (p. 75) *Highbury. . . . Richmond and Kew*: Highbury is a gloomy neighborhood in northeast London. Richmond and Kew are districts on the Thames, west of London. See Eliot's note to line 293. The lines from Dante's *Purgatorio* translate as: 'Remember me, who am La Pia. / Siena made me, Maremma undid me.'

26. (p. 75) *Moorgate*: Station on the London Underground, in the financial district.

27. (p. 75) *Margate Sands*: Seaside resort where Eliot went to recuperate

at the beginning of his breakdown (before traveling to Lausanne) and where he began to compose *The Waste Land*.

28. (p. 76) *Carthage*: Ancient north African city. See Eliot's note to line 307.

29. (p. 76) *Burning burning burning burning*: See Eliot's note to line 308.

30. (p. 76) *O Lord Thou pluckest me out*: See Eliot's note to line 309.

'IV. DEATH BY WATER'

1. (p. 77) *Death by Water*: This section resembles the last lines of 'Dans le Restaurant' from *Poems 1920*.

'V. WHAT THE THUNDER SAID'

1. (p. 78) *What the Thunder Said*: See Eliot's note at the head of his notes to part V.

2. (p. 78) *agony in stony places*: This passage echoes the agony of Christ's betrayal and crucifixion.

3. (p. 78) *Here is no water but only rock*: In a letter to Ford Madox Ford, Eliot called lines 331–358 'the water-dripping song' and said he felt it was the best part of the poem.

4. (p. 79) *hermit-thrush*: See Eliot's note to line 357.

5. (p. 79) *Who is the third who walks always beside you?*: See Eliot's note to line 360.

6. (p. 79) *What is that sound high in the air*: See Eliot's note to line 367–377. Hesse's lines translate as: 'Already half of Europe, already at least half of Eastern Europe, on the way to Chaos, drives drunk in sacred infatuation along the edge of the precipe, sings drunkenly, as though hymn singing, as Dmitri Karamazov [in Dostoevsky's *Brothers Karamazov*] sang. The offended bourgeois laughs at the songs; the saint and the seer hear them with tears.'

7. (p. 80) *Co co rico co co rico*: Alternate rendering of 'cock-a-doodle-doo.'

8. (p. 80) *Ganga*: The River Ganges, in India.

9. (p. 80) *Himavant*: Mountain in the Himalayas.

10. (p. 80) Datta: See Eliot's note to line 402.

11. (p. 80) *the beneficent spider*: See Eliot's note to line 408.

12. (p. 80) *I have heard the key*: See Eliot's note to line 412. Dante's words translate as: 'And I heard below the door of the horrible tower being locked up.'

13. (p. 80) *Coriolanus*: The hero of Shakespeare's play of that title.

14. (p. 81) *Fishing, with the arid plain behind me*: See Eliot's note to line 425.

15. (p. 81) Poi s'ascose nel foco che gli affina: 'Then he stepped back into

the fire which refines.' See Eliot's note to line 428. Dante's lines translate as: 'Now I pray you, by that virtue which guides you to the top of the stairway, be mindful in due time of my pain. Then he stepped back into the fire which refines.'

16. (p. 81) Quando fiam uti chelidon: 'When shall I be like the swallow?' See Eliot's note to line 429.

17. (p. 81) Le Prince d'Aquitaine à la tour abolie: 'The Prince of Aquitaine, to the ruined tower.' See Eliot's note to line 430.

18. (p. 81) *Why then Ile fit you. Hieronymo's mad againe*: See Eliot's note to line 432.

19. (p. 81) *Shantih shantih shantih*: See Eliot's note to line 434.

Inspired by T. S. Eliot
and *The Waste Land*

Poetry, Modernism, and Beyond

In 1965 Robert Lowell said of T. S. Eliot, 'His influence is everywhere inescapable, and nowhere readily usable.' The publication of *The Waste Land* in 1922 introduced a dilemma for America's poets, who were simultaneously inspired and suffocated by Eliot's innovations. Poets as diverse as Ezra Pound, H. D., Hart Crane, William Carlos Williams, Delmore Schwartz, Marianne Moore, Louise Bogan, W. H. Auden, Wallace Stevens, and Robert Penn Warren felt the immediate impact of Eliot. But many found it difficult to respond to his contribution to English verse, one which indisputably demanded acknowledgment. Nonetheless these poets, whether they moved toward Eliot or away from him, strove to respond to his technical advances and his articulation of the horrors of modern life, especially in relation to the 'machine age' and World War I.

In many ways Eliot's *The Waste Land* came to characterize the modernist movement, the dominant literary trend of the early twentieth century. In the essay 'T. S. Eliot as the International Hero' (1945), Delmore Schwartz asserts that Eliot opened up poetry and made in it a space for modern life, just as William Wordsworth made a space in poetry for nature and Marcel Proust made a space in fiction for time. Modernism is seen in the British and American novel as early as the 1890s, notably in the works of Joseph Conrad and Henry James; Proust and James Joyce wrote novels in this style during the years in which Eliot conceived *The Waste Land*; Virginia Woolf reached her peak in the years just following the poem's publication. The modernist novel can be characterized by drastic experiments in the depiction of time and consciousness; a deliberate break from conventions of realism, particularly in relation to plot and representation; and an attention to narrative ambiguity, psychological investigation, deliberate self-consciousness, and frankness about sexual matters. Though poets—chiefly Pound and William Butler Yeats—addressed such issues in the years leading up to *The Waste Land*'s publication, Eliot's poem eclipsed the early moderns in one stroke.

W. H. Auden alludes to Eliot's radical effect on poetry in his poem 'Letter to Lord Byron' (1936), remarking, 'Eliot spoke the still unspoken word.' Louise Bogan, too, felt that Eliot changed the direction of poetry, observing in a 1936 review in the *New Yorker* that 'he swung the balance over from whimpering German bucolics to forms within which contemporary complexity could find expression.' William Carlos Williams felt a strong sense of betrayal by Eliot, particularly on behalf of American poetry, calling *The Waste Land* 'the great catastrophe.' In his 1951 *Autobiography* Williams writes that Eliot 'might have become our adviser, even our hero.' With *The Waste Land*, however, he felt that his fellow poet had turned his back on 'local conditions' and had given the poem 'back to the academics' and old Europe. Williams goes on to recognize Eliot's 'genius' and positive contribution to poetry, especially in metrics, but maintains that the author 'set me back twenty years.'

Ambivalent feelings like those of Lowell, Williams, and others pervade many American poets' evaluations of Eliot. Because of his profound influence over poetry, poets such as Hart Crane sought to distance themselves from Eliot. A great admirer of Eliot, Crane said in a letter dated January 5, 1923, 'My work for the past two years (those meagre drops!) has been more influenced by Eliot than any other modern. . . . However, I take Eliot as a point of departure toward an almost complete reverse of direction. His pessimism is amply justified, in his own case. But I would apply as much of his erudition and technique as I can absorb and assemble toward a more positive . . . ecstatic goal.'

As the twentieth century came to a close, some scholarly evaluations of Eliot attempted to undermine his grip on American poetry. In *The Western Canon: The Books and School of the Ages* (1994), scholar Harold Bloom draws a line of inheritance among American poets: He sees late-twentieth-century writers John Ashbery

and James Merrill as descendants of Wallace Stevens and Eliza-
beth Bishop, who are themselves the 'children' of Emily Dickin-
son; Eliot does not figure into the family tree. In *T. S. Eliot and
American Poetry* (1998), Lee Oser notes that the critic Helen Vendler
began *The Harvard Book of Contemporary American Poetry* (1985)
with twenty-two pages of poems by Wallace Stevens and included
nothing by Eliot, remarking that 'no one was very surprised. After
all, she had long ranked Stevens as the most influential and im-
portant of American modernists.' During his literary career,
Stevens himself tried to ignore Eliot entirely. In a letter dated Jan-
uary 15, 1954, Stevens wrote, 'I am not conscious of having been
influenced by anybody and have purposefully held off from reading
highly mannered people like Eliot and Pound so that I should not
absorb anything, even unconsciously.' Four years earlier, in a letter
dated April 25, 1950, Stevens noted that 'Eliot and I are dead op-
posites and I have been doing about everything that he would not
be likely to do.'

Criticism

Critic F. R. Leavis compares the poetry and criticism of Eliot in his
essay 'T. S. Eliot's Stature as Critic' (1958): 'Eliot's best, his impor-
tant criticism has an immediate relation to his technical problems
as the poet who, at that moment in history, was faced with "altering
expression."' Eliot's writings on literature include *The Sacred Wood*
(1920), *The Use of Poetry and the Use of Criticism* (1933), *Eliza-
bethan Essays* (1934), *Notes Towards the Definition of Culture*
(1948), *Poetry and Drama* (1951), and *On Poetry and Poets* (1957).

Eliot's influence was singular in developing a type of literary in-
vestigation known as New Criticism, which was most influential in
the years 1935–1960, although its legacy extends to the twenty-first
century. Robert Penn Warren was among the early New Critics, a
name that derives from John Crowe Ransom's book *The New Crit-
icism* (1941), which examines the critical work of T. S. Eliot, I. A.
Richards, and William Empson. New Criticism opposes 'extrinsic'
approaches to literature, or those that depend on the biography
and psychology of an author or the historical and sociological

circumstances in which a work is composed. New Critics advocate the 'intrinsic' approach, which exclusively addresses the text and the selection and construction of its language. Today New Criticism alone is considered too limited for scholarly applications, but its principle of close reading continues to contribute heavily to literary studies.

Eliot's essay 'Tradition and the Individual Talent' (1919) prefigures the principles of New Criticism. Rejecting the individualism of Romantics such as John Keats, the essay advances the importance of impersonality in poetry: 'The progress of an artist is a continual self-sacrifice, a continual extinction of personality.' *The Waste Land*, which buries the identity of Eliot with the voices of other authors, demonstrates one possible application of this theory.

In 'Hamlet and His Problems' (1919), Eliot coins the term 'objective correlative.' This phrase and the vague notion of 'dissociation of sensibility,' which appears in his essay 'The Metaphysical Poets' (1921), were discussed extensively in the years following their introduction, though the usefulness of each has been reconsidered since. According to Eliot, a dissociation of sensibility in poets took place after the time of John Donne (1572–1631) and Andrew Marvell (1621–1678). The dissociation was between thoughts and emotions, which were unified under Donne, Marvell, and other metaphysical poets. Eliot felt that poetry beginning with John Milton (1608–1674) and John Dryden (1631–1700) and extending into the nineteenth century lost 'the direct sensuous apprehension of thought' achieved by Donne and Marvell, who were able to convey 'their thought as immediately as the odour of a rose.' In a related vein, and in connection with the concept of the objective correlative, Eliot claims in 'Hamlet and His Problems' that *Hamlet* is an 'artistic failure' because Hamlet does not express his dominant emotion. Eliot writes that 'the only way of expressing emotion in the form of art is by finding an "objective correlative"; in other words, a set of objects, a situation, a chain of events which shall be the formula of that *particular* emotion.'

Eliot's criticism, like his poetry, is not to everyone's liking. The title of Delmore Schwartz's essay 'The Literary Dictatorship of T. S. Eliot' (1949) demonstrates the resentment many readers have felt concerning the prominence of Eliot's ideas. Echoing William

Carlos Williams and Delmore Schwartz, Harold Bloom notes in *The Western Canon*, 'I began my teaching career nearly forty years ago in an academic context dominated by the ideas of T. S. Eliot; ideas that roused me to fury, and against which I fought as vigorously as I could.'

Comments & Questions

In this section, we aim to provide the reader with an array of perspectives on the text, as well as questions that challenge those perspectives. The commentary has been culled from sources as diverse as reviews contemporaneous with the works, letters written by the author, literary criticism of later generations, and appreciations written throughout the works' histories. Following the commentary, a series of questions seeks to filter T. S. Eliot's The Waste Land and Other Poems *through a variety of points of view and bring about a richer understanding of these enduring works.*

Comments

HART CRANE

Eliot's influence threatens to predominate the new English.

—from a letter to Gorham Munson (October 13, 1920)

TIMES LITERARY SUPPLEMENT

Mr. Eliot's poem is also a collection of flashes, but there is no effect of heterogeneity, since all these flashes are relevant to the same thing and together give what seems to be a complete expression of this poet's vision of modern life. We have here range, depth, and beautiful expression. What more is necessary to a great poem? This vision is singularly complex and in all its labyrinths utterly sincere. It is the mystery of life that it shows two faces, and we know of no other modern poet who can more adequately and movingly reveal to us the inextricable tangle of the sordid and the beautiful that make up life. Life is neither hellish nor heavenly; it has a purgatorial quality. And since it is purgatory, deliverance is possible. Students of Mr. Eliot's work will find a new note, and a profoundly interesting one, in the latter part of his poem.

—October 26, 1922

GILBERT SELDES

In essence 'The Waste Land' says something which is not new: that life has become barren and sterile, that man is withering, impotent, and without assurance that the waters which made the land fruitful will ever rise again. (I need not say that 'thoughtful' as the poem is, it does not 'express an idea'; it deals with emotions, and ends precisely in that significant emotion, inherent in the poem, which Mr. Eliot has described.) The title, the plan, and much of the symbolism of the poem, the author tells us in his 'Notes,' were suggested by Miss Weston's remarkable book on the Grail legend, 'From Ritual to Romance'; it is only indispensable to know that there exists the legend of a king rendered impotent, and his country sterile, both awaiting deliverance by a knight on his way to seek the Grail; it is interesting to know further that this is part of the Life or Fertility mysteries; but the poem is self-contained. It seems at first sight remarkably disconnected, confused, the emotion seems to disengage itself in spite of the objects and events chosen by the poet as their vehicle. . . .

A closer view of the poem does more than illuminate the difficulties; it reveals the hidden form of the work, indicates how each thing falls into place, and to the reader's surprise shows that the emotion which at first seemed to come in spite of the framework and the detail could not otherwise have been communicated. For the theme is not a distaste for life, nor is it a disillusion, a romantic pessimism of any kind. It is specifically concerned with the idea of the Waste Land—that the land *was* fruitful and now is not, that life had been rich, beautiful, assured, organized, lofty, and now is dragging itself out in a poverty-stricken, and disrupted and ugly tedium, without health, and with no consolation in morality; there may remain for the poet the labor of poetry, but in the poem there remain only 'these fragments I have shored against my ruins'—the broken glimpses of what was. The poem is not an argument and I can only add, to be fair, that it contains no romantic idealization of the past; one feels simply that even in the cruelty and madness which have left their record in history and in art, there was an intensity of life, a germination and fruitfulness, which are now gone, and that even the creative imagination, even hallucination and vision have atrophied, so that water shall never again be struck from a rock in the desert. Mr. Bertrand Russell has recently said that since the Renaissance the clock of Europe has been running down; without the feeling that it was once wound up, without the contrasting emotions as one looks at the past and at the present, 'The Waste Land' would be a different poem, and the problem of the poem would have been solved another way.

—from *The Nation* (December 6, 1922)

EDMUND WILSON

Mr. Eliot is a poet. It is true his poems seem the products of a constricted emotional experience and that he appears to have drawn rather heavily on books for the heat he could not derive from life. There is a certain grudging margin, to be sure, about all that Mr. Eliot writes—as if he were compensating himself for his limitations by a peevish assumption of superiority. But it is the very acuteness of his suffering from his starvation which gives such poignancy to his art. And, as I say, Mr. Eliot is a poet—that is, he feels intensely and with distinction and speaks naturally in beautiful verse—so that, no matter within what walls he lives, he belongs to the divine company. His verse is sometimes much too scrappy—he does not dwell long enough upon one idea to give it its proportionate value before passing to the next—but these drops, though they be wrung from flint, are none the less authentic crystals. They are broken and sometimes infinitely tiny, but they are worth all the rhinestones on the market. I doubt whether there is a single other poem of equal length by a contemporary American which displays so high and so varied a mastery of English verse. The poem is—in spite of its lack of structural unity—simply one triumph after another—from the white April light of the opening and the sweet wistfulness of the nightingale passage—one of the only successful pieces of contemporary blank verse—to the shabby sadness of the Thames Maidens, the cruel irony of Tiresias' vision, and the dry grim stony style of the descriptions of the Waste Land itself.

That is why Mr. Eliot's trivialities are more valuable than other people's epics—why Mr. Eliot's detestation of Sweeney is more precious than Mr. Sandburg's sympathy for him, and Mr. Prufrock's tea-table tragedy more important than all the passions of the New Adam—sincere and carefully expressed as these latter emotions indubitably are. That is also why, for all its complicated correspondences and its recondite references and quotations, *The Waste Land* is intelligible at first reading. It is not necessary to know anything about the Grail Legend or any but the most obvious of Mr. Eliot's allusions to feel the force of the intense emotion which the poem is intended to convey—as one cannot do, for example, with the extremely ill-focused *Eight Cantos* of his imitator Mr. Ezra Pound, who presents only a bewildering mosaic with no central emotion to provide a key. In Eliot the very images and the sound of the words—even when we do not know precisely why he has chosen them—are charged with a strange poignancy which seems to bring us into the heart of a singer. And sometimes we feel that he is speaking not only for a personal distress, but for the starvation of a whole civilization—for people grinding at barren office-routine in the cells of gigantic cities, drying up their souls in eternal toil whose products never bring them profit, where their pleasures are so vulgar and so feeble that they are almost sadder than their pains. It is our whole world of strained nerves and shattered institutions, in which 'some infinitely gentle, infinitely suffering thing' is somehow being done to death—in which the maiden Philomel 'by the barbarous king so rudely forced' can no longer even fill the desert 'with inviolable voice.' It is the world in which the pursuit of grace and beauty is something which is felt to be obsolete—the reflections which reach us from the past cannot illumine so dingy a scene; that heroic prelude has ironic echoes among the streets and the drawing-rooms where we live. Yet the race of the poets—though grown rarer—is not yet quite dead: there is at least one who, as Mr. Pound says, has brought a new personal rhythm into the language and who has lent even to the words of the great predecessors a new music and a new meaning.

—from *The Dial* (December 1922)

CONRAD AIKEN

In 'The Waste Land,' Mr. Eliot's sense of the literary past has become so overmastering as almost to constitute the motive of the work. It is as if, in conjunction with Mr. Pound of the 'Cantos,' he wanted to make a 'literature of literature'—a poetry not more actuated by life itself than by poetry.

—from the *New Republic* (February 7, 1923)

WILLIAM BUTLER YEATS

I think of [Eliot] as satirist rather than poet.

—from *The Oxford Book of Modern Verse* (1936)

RALPH ELLISON

Wuthering Heights had caused me an agony of inexpressible emotion and the same was true of *Jude the Obscure*, but *The Waste Land* seized my mind. I was intrigued by its power to move me while eluding my understanding. Somehow its rhythms were often closer to those of jazz than were those of the Negro poets, and even though I could not understand then, its range of allusion was as mixed and as varied as that of Louis Armstrong.

—from *Shadow and Act* (1964)

ROBERT FROST

Eliot and I have our similarities and our differences. We are both poets and we both like to play. That's the similarity. The difference is this: I like to play euchre. He likes to play Eucharist.

—from *The Letters of Robert Frost to Louis Untermeyer* (1963)

R. W. B. LEWIS

Edith Wharton found . . . [*Prufrock*] extremely 'amusing' . . . but relatively insignificant and interesting mainly as revealing the influence of Whitman. . . . *The Waste Land* . . . seemed to her to lack even the enlivening presence of Walt Whitman; it was a poem, like Joyce's novel [*Ulysses*] ridden by theory rather than warmed by life.

—R. W. B. Lewis, *Edith Wharton* (1975)

JOHN BERRYMAN

'Like a patient etherised upon a table . . .' With this line, modern poetry begins.

—from *The Freedom of the Poet* (1976)

Questions

1. (a) *The Waste Land* poses a God-awful present against a wonderful past. (b) *The Waste Land* depicts a past as awful as the present.

(c) *The Waste Land* is not a poem about how things are or were, but a poem about perspective, about how the present sees itself and the past.
Which of these assertions is closest to the truth?

2. How would you characterize the depiction of sex (or love or the relations between the sexes) in *The Waste Land*?

3. Do Eliot's notes on *The Waste Land* strike you as a put-on, as showing off, as genuinely informative, as typical of Eliot's pedantic personality, as all these at once?

4. How is Madame Sosostris related to anything else in the poem? Ask yourself the same question about Phlebas the Phoenician.

5. It is often said that *The Waste Land* is a crucial event in the 'Modernist' movement, and that its methods and interests are the literary equivalent of methods and interests in the works of, say, Picasso and Stravinsky. From what you know about these other artists, is this categorization of Eliot's work valid?

For Further Reading

Biography

Gordon, Lyndall. *T. S. Eliot: An Imperfect Life*. London: Vintage, 1998. Exhaustive and highly regarded study of Eliot's life and career.

Critical Studies

Asher, Kenneth. *T. S. Eliot and Ideology*. Cambridge and New York: Cambridge University Press, 1995. Demonstrates the effect of politics on Eliot's work, with attention to the influence of French reactionary thinking.

Brooker, Jewel Spears. *Mastery and Escape: T. S. Eliot and the Dialectic of Modernism*. Amherst: University of Massachusetts Press, 1994. Analyzes modernism as a cultural and literary phenomenon and as an ideology, focusing on Eliot and his relations to Mallarmé, Hulme, Yeats, and Joyce.

Bush, Ronald. *T. S. Eliot: A Study in Character and Style*. New York: Oxford University Press, 1984. Argues that Eliot's character was torn by the same conflict that charged his poetry—an intense tension between romantic yearning and intellectual detachment.

Chinitz, David. *T. S. Eliot and the Cultural Divide*. Chicago: University of Chicago Press, 2003. Examines Eliot's engagement with popular culture, such as American jazz, and finds that his attitude toward such culture is surprisingly less hostile than has been generally assumed.

Julius, Anthony. *T. S. Eliot: Anti-Semitism and Literary Form*. New York: Thames and Hudson, 2003. Controversial study of Eliot's deployment of anti-Semitic discourse and the role it played in his literary works.

Kenner, Hugh. *The Invisible Poet*. 1959. New York: Harcourt, 1969. An old but classic account of Eliot's career, by one of the liveliest writers in the field.

119

Malamud, Randy. *The Language of Modernism*. Ann Arbor, MI: UMI Research Press, 1989. Explains why modernist literature looks the way it does, and how readers may learn to understand the language, style, and tropes of Eliot, Woolf, and Joyce.

Menand, Louis. *Discovering Modernism: T. S. Eliot and His Context*. Oxford: Oxford University Press, 1992. Intellectual history of Eliot and the role he played in the rise of literary modernism.

Moody, Anthony David. *Tracing T. S. Eliot's Spirit: Essays on His Poetry and Thought*. Cambridge and New York: Cambridge University Press, 1996. Discusses Eliot's quest for the world of the spirit, with attention to the religions and cultures of America, India, and Europe.

North, Michael. *Reading 1922: A Return to the Scene of the Modern*. New York and Oxford: Oxford University Press, 1999. Discusses the cultural climate of the year in which *The Waste Land* and *Ulysses* were published, *The Great Gatsby* was set, the Fascists took over in Italy, the Irish Free State was born, the Harlem Renaissance reached its peak, and Charlie Chaplin's popularity peaked.

Sigg, Eric. *The American T. S. Eliot: A Study of the Early Writings*. Cambridge and New York: Cambridge University Press, 1989. Discusses the significance of Eliot's American heritage, which is often overlooked; elucidates links between Eliot's work and that of Henry James, Henry Adams, and George Santayana.

Skaff, William. *The Philosophy of T. S. Eliot: From Skepticism to a Surrealist Poetic, 1909–1927*. Philadelphia: University of Pennsylvania Press, 1986. A study of the philosophical backdrop to Eliot's life and poetry.

Svarny, Erik. *'The Men of 1914': T. S. Eliot and Early Modernism*. Milton Keynes, U.K., and Philadelphia, PA: Open University Press, 1988. Examines Eliot's work in relation to his contemporaries, especially Ezra Pound, Wyndham Lewis, and T. E. Hulme.

Essay Collections

Brooker, Jewel Spears, ed. *T. S. Eliot and Our Turning World*. New York: St. Martin's Press, 2001. Essay topics include 'Shakespeare/Dante and Water/Music in *The Waste Land*,' 'T. S. Eliot and the Feminist Revision of the Modern(ist) Canon,' 'Buddhist Epistemology in T. S. Eliot's Theory of Poetry,' and 'T. S. Eliot and Heraclitus.'

Bush, Ronald, ed. *T. S. Eliot: The Modernist in History.* Cambridge and New York: Cambridge University Press, 1991. Essay topics include 'Eliot's Women/Women's Eliot,' 'The Price of Modernism: Publishing *The Waste Land*,' 'The Allusive Poet: Eliot and His Sources,' and '*Ara Vos Prec*: Eliot's Negotiation of Satire and Suffering.'

Olney, James, ed. *T. S. Eliot: Essays from the Southern Review.* Oxford: Clarendon Press, 1988. Essay topics include 'Eliot at Oxford,' 'The Significance of T. S. Eliot's Philosophical Notebooks,' 'Substitutes for Christianity in the Poetry of T. S. Eliot,' and several personal reminiscences.

Readers' Guide

Southam, B. C. *A Guide to the Selected Poems of T. S. Eliot.* Sixth edition; first U.S. edition. New York: Harcourt Brace, 1996. A comprehensive overview with extensive annotations.

Critical Editions

Eliot, Valerie, ed. *The Waste Land: A Facsimile and Transcript of the Original Drafts Including the Annotations of Ezra Pound.* New York: Harcourt Brace Jovanovich, 1971. Reproduces drafts of *The Waste Land*, showing the editing done by Ezra Pound and discussing the history of the poem's composition and publication.

Ricks, Christopher, ed. *Inventions of the March Hare: Poems, 1909–1917.* New York: Harcourt Brace, 1996. Presents numerous drafts of Eliot's early work, published and previously unpublished, with discussion of the poems' evolution.

Other Works Cited in the Introduction

Eliot, T. S. 'Tradition and the Individual Talent.' 1919. Reprinted in Eliot's *The Sacred Wood: Essays on Poetry and Criticism.* London: Methuen, 1920.

——. 'Hamlet and His Problems.' 1919. Reprinted in Eliot's *The Sacred Wood: Essays on Poetry and Criticism.* London: Methuen, 1920.

——. *Dante.* London: Faber and Faber, 1929.

Look for the following titles, available now and forthcoming from
BARNES & NOBLE CLASSICS.

Visit your local bookstore for these and more fine titles.
Or to order online go to: WWW.BN.COM/CLASSICS

Title	Author	ISBN	Price
Aesop's Fables	Aesop	1-59308-062-X	$5.95
The Age of Innocence	Edith Wharton	1-59308-143-X	$5.95
Agnes Grey	Anne Brontë	1-59308-323-8	$5.95
Alice's Adventures in Wonderland and Through the Looking-Glass	Lewis Carroll	1-59308-015-8	$5.95
Anna Karenina	Leo Tolstoy	1-59308-027-1	$8.95
The Art of War	Sun Tzu	1-59308-017-4	$7.95
The Awakening and Selected Short Fiction	Kate Chopin	1-59308-113-8	$6.95
Babbitt	Sinclair Lewis	1-59308-267-3	$7.95
Barchester Towers	Anthony Trollope	1-59308-337-8	$7.95
The Beautiful and Damned	F. Scott Fitzgerald	1-59308-245-2	$7.95
Beowulf	Anonymous	1-59308-266-5	$4.95
Bleak House	Charles Dickens	1-59308-311-4	$9.95
The Bostonians	Henry James	1-59308-297-5	$7.95
The Brothers Karamazov	Fyodor Dostoevsky	1-59308-045-X	$9.95
The Call of the Wild and White Fang	Jack London	1-59308-200-2	$5.95
Candide	Voltaire	1-59308-028-X	$4.95
A Christmas Carol, The Chimes and The Cricket on the Hearth	Charles Dickens	1-59308-033-6	$5.95
The Collected Poems of Emily Dickinson	Emily Dickinson	1-59308-050-6	$5.95
Common Sense and Other Writings	Thomas Paine	1-59308-209-6	$6.95
The Communist Manifesto and Other Writings	Karl Marx and Friedrich Engels	1-59308-100-6	$5.95
The Complete Sherlock Holmes, Vol. I	Sir Arthur Conan Doyle	1-59308-034-4	$7.95
The Complete Sherlock Holmes, Vol. II	Sir Arthur Conan Doyle	1-59308-040-9	$7.95
A Connecticut Yankee in King Arthur's Court	Mark Twain	1-59308-210-X	$7.95
The Count of Monte Cristo	Alexandre Dumas	1-59308-151-0	$7.95
The Country of the Pointed Firs and Selected Short Fiction	Sarah Orne Jewett	1-59308-262-2	$6.95
Daisy Miller and Washington Square	Henry James	1-59308-105-7	$4.95
Daniel Deronda	George Eliot	1-59308-290-8	$8.95
David Copperfield	Charles Dickens	1-59308-063-8	$7.95
Dead Souls	Nikolai Gogol	1-59308-092-1	$7.95
The Death of Ivan Ilych and Other Stories	Leo Tolstoy	1-59308-069-7	$7.95
The Deerslayer	James Fenimore Cooper	1-59308-211-8	$7.95
Don Quixote	Miguel de Cervantes	1-59308-046-8	$9.95
Dracula	Bram Stoker	1-59308-114-6	$6.95
Emma	Jane Austen	1-59308-152-9	$6.95
The Enchanted Castle and Five Children and It	Edith Nesbit	1-59308-274-6	$6.95
Essays and Poems by Ralph Waldo Emerson		1-59308-076-X	$6.95
Essential Dialogues of Plato		1-59308-269-X	$9.95
The Essential Tales and Poems of Edgar Allan Poe		1-59308-064-6	$7.95
Ethan Frome and Selected Stories	Edith Wharton	1-59308-090-5	$5.95

(continued)

(continued)

Title	Author	ISBN	Price
Sister Carrie	Theodore Dreiser	1-59308-226-6	$7.95
Six Plays by Henrik Ibsen		1-59308-061-1	$8.95
Sons and Lovers	D. H. Lawrence	1-59308-013-1	$7.95
The Souls of Black Folk	W. E. B. Du Bois	1-59308-014-X	$5.95
The Strange Case of Dr. Jekyll and Mr. Hyde and Other Stories	Robert Louis Stevenson	1-59308-131-6	$4.95
Swann's Way	Marcel Proust	1-59308-295-9	$8.95
A Tale of Two Cities	Charles Dickens	1-59308-138-3	$5.95
Tao Te Ching	Lao Tzu	1-59308-256-8	$5.95
Tess of d'Urbervilles	Thomas Hardy	1-59308-228-2	$7.95
This Side of Paradise	F. Scott Fitzgerald	1-59308-243-6	$6.95
Three Lives	Gertrude Stein	1-59308-320-3	$6.95
The Three Musketeers	Alexandre Dumas	1-59308-148-0	$8.95
Thus Spoke Zarathustra	Friedrich Nietzsche	1-59308-278-9	$7.95
Tom Jones	Henry Fielding	1-59308-070-0	$8.95
Treasure Island	Robert Louis Stevenson	1-59308-247-9	$4.95
The Turn of the Screw, The Aspern Papers and Two Stories	Henry James	1-59308-043-3	$5.95
Twenty Thousand Leagues Under the Sea	Jules Verne	1-59308-302-5	$5.95
Uncle Tom's Cabin	Harriet Beecher Stowe	1-59308-121-9	$7.95
Utopia	Sir Thomas More	1-59308-244-4	$5.95
Vanity Fair	William Makepeace Thackeray	1-59308-071-9	$7.95
The Varieties of Religious Experience	William James	1-59308-072-7	$7.95
Villette	Charlotte Brontë	1-59308-316-5	$7.95
The Virginian	Owen Wister	1-59308-236-3	$7.95
The Voyage Out	Virginia Woolf	1-59308-229-0	$6.95
Walden and Civil Disobedience	Henry David Thoreau	1-59308-208-8	$5.95
War and Peace	Leo Tolstoy	1-59308-073-5	$12.95
Ward No. 6 and Other Stories	Anton Chekhov	1-59308-003-4	$7.95
The Waste Land and Other Poems	T. S. Eliot	1-59308-279-7	$4.95
The Way We Live Now	Anthony Trollope	1-59308-304-1	$9.95
The Wind in the Willows	Kenneth Grahame	1-59308-265-7	$4.95
The Wings of the Dove	Henry James	1-59308-296-7	$7.95
Wives and Daughters	Elizabeth Gaskell	1-59308-257-6	$7.95
The Woman in White	Wilkie Collins	1-59308-280-0	$7.95
Women in Love	D. H. Lawrence	1-59308-258-4	$8.95
The Wonderful Wizard of Oz	L. Frank Baum	1-59308-221-5	$6.95
Wuthering Heights	Emily Brontë	1-59308-128-6	$5.95

Ɓ
BARNES & NOBLE CLASSICS

If you are an educator and would like to receive an
Examination or Desk Copy of a Barnes & Noble Classic edition,
please refer to Academic Resources on our website at
WWW.BN.COM/CLASSICS
or contact us at
B&NCLASSICS@BN.COM.

All prices are subject to change.

0106